THE WIND THAT LAYS WASTE

THE WIND THAT LAYS WASTE

A Novel

Selva Almada

Translated from the Spanish by Chris Andrews

Graywolf Press

This publication is made possible, in part, by the voters of Minnesota through a Minnesota State Arts Board Operating Support grant, thanks to a legislative appropriation from the arts and cultural heritage fund. Significant support has also been provided by Target, the McKnight Foundation, the Lannan Foundation, the Amazon Literary Partnership, and other generous contributions from foundations, corporations, and individuals. To these organizations and individuals we offer our heartfelt thanks.

Work published within the framework of "Sur" Translation Support Program of the Ministry of Foreign Affairs and Worship of the Argentine Republic. Obra editada en el marco del Programa "Sur" de Apoyo a las Traducciones del Ministerio de Relaciones Exteriores y Culto de la República Argentina.

Published by Graywolf Press
250 Third Avenue North, Suite 600
Minneapolis, Minnesota 55401

www.graywolfpress.org

Published in the United States of America

ISBN 978-1-55597-845-7

2 4 6 8 9 7 5 3 1
First Graywolf Printing, 2019

Library of Congress Control Number: 2018958169

Cover design: Kimberly Glyder

Cover art: Shutterstock

THE WIND THAT LAYS WASTE

The wind brings the thirst of all these years.
The wind brings every winter's hunger.
The wind brings the clamor of the ravines, the clamor of the fields and
the desert.
The wind brings the cries of women and men fed up with the crumbs
from the bosses' table.
The wind comes with the force of a new era.
The wind roars, and twisters go whirling over the earth.
We are the wind and the fire that will lay waste to the world with the
love of Christ.

1

The mechanic coughed and spat out a gob of phlegm.

"My lungs are shot," he said, wiping his mouth with his hand and bending down again under the open hood.

The owner of the car mopped his brow with a handkerchief and bent down too so their heads were side by side. He adjusted his wire-rimmed spectacles and contemplated the jumble of hot metal parts. Then he looked at the mechanic inquiringly.

"Can you fix it?"

"I reckon so."

"How long will it take?"

The mechanic straightened up—he was almost a foot taller—and looked at the sky. It was getting on for midday.

"End of the afternoon, I reckon."

"We'll have to wait here."

"If you like. It's all pretty basic here, as you can see."

"We'd rather wait. Maybe you'll be done early, with God's help."

The mechanic shrugged and took a pack of cigarettes from his shirt pocket. He offered one to the car's owner.

"No, no, I quit years ago, thank God. If you don't mind me saying so, you should too . . ."

"The soda machine isn't working, but there should be some cans in the fridge, if you're thirsty."

"Thanks."

"Tell the young lady to get out of the car. She's going to roast in there."

"What was your name?"

"Brauer. El Gringo Brauer. And that's Tapioca, my assistant."

"I'm Reverend Pearson."

They shook hands.

"I've got a few things to do before I can start work on your car."

"Go ahead, please. Don't mind us. God bless you."

The Reverend went around to the back of the car where his daughter, Leni, was sulking in the tiny space left by the boxes full of Bibles and the piles of magazines on the seats and the floor. He tapped on the window. Leni looked at him through the dusty glass. He tried the handle, but she had locked the door. He gestured to tell her to wind the window down. She lowered it an inch or two.

"It's going to take a while to fix. Get out, Leni. We'll have a cool drink."

"I'm fine here."

"It's very hot, sweetheart. You're going to get heatstroke."

Leni wound up the window again.

The Reverend opened the passenger door, reached in to unlock the back door, and pulled it open.

"Elena, get out."

He held on to the door until she obeyed. And as soon as she was out of the way, he slammed it shut.

The girl rearranged her skirt, which was sticky with sweat, and looked at the mechanic, who acknowledged her with a nod. A boy who must have been about her age, sixteen, was watching them, wide-eyed.

Her father introduced the older man as Mr. Brauer. He was

very tall, with a red mustache like a horseshoe that came down almost to his chin; he was wearing a pair of oily jeans and a shirt that was open, exposing his chest, but tucked in. He would have been over fifty, but there was something youthful about him; it must have been the mustache and the long hair, hanging down to his collar. The boy was wearing old jeans too, patched but clean, and a faded T-shirt and sandals. His straight, jet-black hair had been neatly cut, and he looked like he hadn't started shaving. Both of them were thin, but they had the sinewy bodies of those accustomed to the use of brute force.

Fifty yards away stood the makeshift building that served as gas station, garage, and home: a single room of bare bricks beyond the old pump, with one door and one window. In front of it, at an angle, a kind of porch, with an awning made of branches and reeds, which shaded a small table, a stack of plastic chairs, and the soda machine. A dog was sleeping in the dirt under the table. When it heard them approach, it opened one yellow eye and swished its tail on the ground without getting up.

"Give them something to drink," said Brauer to the boy, who took two chairs from the stack and wiped them with a rag so that they could sit down.

"What do you want, sweetheart?"

"A Coke."

"A glass of water's fine for me. The biggest one you have, son," said the Reverend as he sat down.

The boy stepped through the curtain of plastic strips and disappeared inside.

"The car will be ready by the end of the afternoon, God willing," said the Reverend, mopping his brow again.

"And if he's not willing?" Leni replied, putting on the earphones of the Walkman that was permanently attached to her belt. She hit Play, and her head filled with music.

A big heap of scrap reared beside the house, extending almost to the shoulder of the road: panels, bits of agricultural machinery, wheel rims, piles of tires; a real cemetery of chassis, axles, and twisted bits of metal, immobilized forever under the scorching sun.

2

After several weeks of touring around Entre Ríos—they had come down from the north along the Río Uruguay to Concordia, then taken Highway 18 right through the middle of the province to Paraná—the Reverend decided to go on to Chaco.

They spent a couple of days in Paraná, the city where he had been born. Although he no longer had relatives or acquaintances there, having left when he was very young, he liked to go back every now and then.

They stayed in a run-down hotel near the old bus terminal: a poky, depressing place with a view of the red-light district. Leni amused herself watching the weary comings and goings of the prostitutes and transvestites, who wore so little they barely had to undress when a client turned up. With his nose in his books and papers as usual, the Reverend was completely oblivious to their surroundings.

Although he couldn't bring himself to visit his grandparents' house, where his mother had brought him into the world and raised him on her own (his father, a North American adventurer, had vanished before his birth, along with the in-laws' meager savings), he took Leni to see an old park on the banks of the river.

They walked among ancient trees and saw the watermarks on their trunks, very high up on the ones near the bank; some still had flood wrack in their top branches. They ate their lunch on a stone table, and the Reverend said that as a child he'd come to that park several times with his mother.

"It was very different then," he said, and bit into a sandwich. "On the weekends it was full of people. Not run-down like this."

As he ate, he looked nostalgically at the broken benches, the long grass, and the trash left by visitors the previous weekend.

When they finished their lunch, the Reverend wanted to go farther into the park; he said that there used to be two swimming pools and he was curious to see if they were still there. It didn't take long to find them. Bits of iron were visible in the cracked cement around the edges; the tiles covering the inside walls were smeared with mud, and some were missing here and there, as if the old pools were losing their teeth. The floors were miniature swamps, breeding grounds for mosquitoes and toads, which hid among the plants growing in the slime.

The Reverend sighed. The days were long gone when he and other children his age would bounce off the diving board into the water, planting their feet on the tiled floor and pushing back up to break the bright surface with their heads.

He put his hands in his pockets and started walking slowly along the edge of one of the pools, head hanging and shoulders slumped. Leni watched her father's bowed back and felt a bit sorry for him. She guessed that he was remembering happier times, the days of his childhood, the summer afternoons he'd spent there.

But her compassion didn't last. He could at least go back to places full of memories. He could recognize a tree and reconstruct the day when he and his friends had climbed it right to the top. He could remember his mother spreading a checkered cloth over one of those ruined tables. But Leni had no lost paradise to revisit. Her childhood was very recent, but her memory of it was empty. Thanks to her father, the Reverend Pearson, and his holy mission, all she could remember was the inside of the same old car, crummy rooms in hundreds of indistinguishable hotels, the features of dozens of children she never spent long enough with to miss when the time came to move on, and a mother whose face she could hardly recall.

The Reverend completed his circuit and came back to where his daughter was still standing, as rigid as Lot's wife, as pitiless as the seven plagues.

Leni saw his eyes glistening and quickly turned her back on him.

"Let's go, Father. This place stinks."

3

Tapioca came back with a bottle of Coke for Leni and a glass of water for the Reverend. He handed them the drinks and stood there like an overattentive waiter.

Pearson drank the whole glass down in one gulp. In spite of its warmth and dubious color, the Reverend received that water as if it had flowed from the purest spring. If God put it on earth, it must be good, he always said.

He gave the empty glass back to the mechanic's assistant, who gripped it with both hands, unsure what to do with it. He kept shifting his weight from one foot to the other.

"Do you go to church, son?" asked the Reverend.

Tapioca shook his head and looked down, ashamed.

"But you're a Christian."

The boy stopped shifting his weight and stood there staring at the tips of his sandals.

There was a gleam in the Reverend's eyes. He got up, walked over to Tapioca, and stood in front of him. He bent down a little, trying to see the boy's face.

"Are you baptized?"

Tapioca looked up and the Reverend saw himself reflected in

his large, dark eyes, which were moist like the eyes of a fawn. A flicker of curiosity made the boy's pupils contract.

"Tapioca," Brauer called out. "Here. I need you here."

The boy gave the glass back to the Reverend and ran over to his boss. Pearson raised the greasy vessel and smiled. His mission on earth was to wash dirty souls, to make them sparkling clean again, and fill them with the word of God.

"Leave him alone," said Leni, who had been watching the scene with interest as she sipped her Coke.

"God puts us exactly where we ought to be, Elena."

"We ought to be at Pastor Zack's place, Father."

"And we will be, after."

"After what?"

Her father didn't answer. And she didn't insist; she didn't want to get into a quarrel or know anything about his mysterious plans.

She watched as Brauer gave Tapioca some orders and the boy climbed up into the cabin of an old truck. He steered while the Gringo strained to push the vehicle to a tree about two hundred yards away, where he left it in the shade.

When the truck was where he wanted it, he collapsed onto the bare earth with his arms flung out and his mouth hanging open, gasping hot air into his lungs. The way his heart was beating in his chest, it felt like a cat in a bag. He looked up at the fragments of sky visible through the sparse canopy of leaves.

Once, Brauer had been a very strong man. At the age of twenty, he would put a chain over his bare shoulders and tow a tractor, easily, just to amuse his friends.

Now he was three decades older, a mere shadow of the young Hercules who used to enjoy displaying his phenomenal strength.

Tapioca bent down over him.

"Hey, boss. You okay?"

Brauer lifted an arm to reassure the kid but still couldn't say a word; he could barely gather enough strength to smile and give him a thumbs-up.

Tapioca laughed with relief and ran back to the service station to get some water.

Out of the corner of his eye, the Gringo saw his helper's sandals raising dust, the boy running knock-kneed, awkwardly, as if he were still a child, not almost a man.

He looked up again at the sky, broken into pieces by the tree. His shirt was soaked, and he could feel the sweat gathering in his navel, then overflowing and running down either side of his belly. Little by little his breathing slowed, and his heart stopped jumping around in his rib cage, returning to its normal place within the frame of bones. His body was seized by the first spasm of a cough, which made him sit up suddenly and filled his mouth with phlegm. He spat it all out, as far as he could. Then he felt for a cigarette and lit it.

4

After walking around the park where he used to go as a child, the Reverend found a telephone booth to call Pastor Zack. It was a comfort to hear his voice. He was a good friend, and it had been almost three years since they had seen each other.

"My dear friend, the Lord be praised," thundered Zack at the other end of the line.

Zack was a cheerful, ebullient man; it was always good to have him near.

"The good Lord smiles when he hears you laugh," the Reverend always said to him, and Zack would erupt into one of his Cossack guffaws, the only relic of his drinking days, for the Pastor had known how to drink like the good Cossack he was. But he had left all that behind him, with the help of Christ. Sometimes he would look at his big, square hands, strong as a pair of power shovels. They were raising the beams of a temple now, but those hands had once beaten women. When Zack remembered that, he would break down and cry like a child, letting his hands hang limp at his sides, not daring to lift them to his face, for fear their past might taint his remorse.

"I'd cut them off if I could," he had once told the Reverend, "but they'd be poison, even for a dog."

The Reverend had taken those hands in his and kissed them. "These hands are fit to wash the feet of Christ," he had said.

They spoke for a while on the telephone, exchanging their latest news. Pastor Zack and his wife, Ofelia, had a new child, their fourth: a boy named Jonás. But what the Pastor was really excited about was the completion of the temple. Another beacon for Christ, deep in the forest, near Río Bermejito, in an indigenous community.

Zack chattered on without pause. Sitting on the little bench in the booth, the Reverend nodded and smiled, as if visible to his interlocutor. At one point, when the Pastor cried out and struck the table, the sound of it was so clear that Zack seemed to be right there beside him.

"But of course," he said, "you have to come. It will be a great honor. My temple, our temple, won't be properly finished until you step into the pulpit. When you start to preach, even the forest birds will be quiet. And I tell you, they *never* shut up here, blessed little creatures, even when they're sleeping. I won't let you say no. Ah, Reverend, my heart is pounding. You'll come, won't you? Say you will. Ofelia, Ofelia," called the Pastor.

"Yes, of course I'll come, but I have to sort a few things out," stammered the Reverend.

"The Lord be praised! What wonderful news! Ofelia, Pearson is coming to visit, isn't that great?" Zack burst out laughing. "Ofelia's so happy she's dancing; if only you could see her. She's teaching the children here to sing; wait till you hear them, it's such a sweet choir. Leni could sing too. You'll bring her, won't you? Ofelia, Leni's coming too, bless her. Ofelia adores her. Is she there? I'd like to say hello."

"No, no, Leni's not here now, but I'll tell her you said hello. She'll be happy to see you both too."

They talked awhile longer, and the Reverend promised to get there in the next few days.

Reverend Pearson is an outstanding preacher. His sermons are always something to remember, and within his church he is held in high regard.

Whenever the Reverend steps onto the stage—and he always appears abruptly, as if he had been wrestling with the Devil, who had tried to bar his way—everyone falls silent.

The Reverend bows his head and raises his arms slightly, with the palms facing forward, then facing up. He remains like that for a moment, showing the faithful his bald crown, beaded with sweat. When he lifts his head, he takes two steps forward and looks at his audience. The way he looks, you know he's looking at you, even if you're sitting in the back row. (It's Christ who's looking at you!) He begins to speak. (Christ's tongue is moving in his mouth!) His arms begin to perform their choreography of gestures, only the hands moving at first, slowly, as if they were caressing the listeners' weary brows. (Christ's fingertips on my temples!) Gradually his forearms and upper arms begin to move as well. The torso remains still, but already you can sense a movement in his stomach. (It's the flame of Christ burning inside him!) He glides to one side: one, two, three steps, index fingers extended, pointing at everyone and no one. He comes back to the center: four, five, six. And now he's gliding—seven, eight, nine—across to the other side. His index fingers point at everyone and no one. (It's Christ's finger pointing at you!) Then he comes back to the center again and begins to walk down the aisle. Now his legs join the dance. His whole body is moving, even his toes under the shoe leather. He strips off his jacket and tie. All this without ever ceasing to speak. Because from the moment he lifted his head and looked at the audience, Christ's tongue has moved in his mouth and will not cease to move. He walks up and down the aisle, goes to the door, and retraces his steps; his eyes are shut and his arms flung wide, his hands moving like radar seeking out the most wretched of all. The Reverend does not need to see. When the moment comes, Christ will tell him who should be taken up onto the stage.

He reaches out at random and grasps the wrist of a woman who is crying and shaking like a leaf. Although the woman feels that her limbs are not responding, the Reverend takes hold of her and sweeps her up like a leaf in the wind. He places her at the front of the stage. The woman is sixty years old; her stomach is bulging as if she were pregnant. The Reverend kneels in front of her. He rests his face against her belly. Now, for the first time, he stops speaking. His mouth opens. The woman can feel the open mouth, the Reverend's teeth biting the fabric of her dress. The Reverend writhes. The little bones of his spine move like a snake under his shirt. The woman can't stop crying. Her tears are mixed with snot and drool. She opens her arms; her flesh sags. The woman cries out and all the others cry with her. The Reverend stands up and turns toward the congregation. His face is red and sweaty, and there is something caught between his teeth. It is slimy and black. He spits it out: a scrap of fabric that reeks of the Devil.

5

"Let us give thanks," said the Reverend.

Tapioca and the Gringo froze, their food-laden forks halfway between plate and mouth.

"If you don't mind," said the Reverend.

"Go ahead."

The Reverend clasped his hands and rested them on the edge of the table. Leni did the same and lowered her eyes. Tapioca looked at the Gringo and the guests, then put his hands together too. Brauer's remained apart, one on either side of his plate.

"Lord, bless this food and this table. Thank you, Jesus, for giving us the opportunity to meet these friends. Praised be thy name."

The Reverend smiled.

"Okay," he said.

The four of them dug into the food: lots of rice and a few pieces of cold meat left over from last night's dinner. They were all hungry, so for a while there was only the sound of the cutlery against the glazed plates. Tapioca and Brauer ate in a rush, as if they were racing to see who would finish first. The Reverend and Leni were slower. He had taught her that it was important to chew your food well before swallowing: good chewing is an aid to good digestion.

"Have you been living here long?" Pearson asked.

"Fair while," said the Gringo, swallowing and wiping his mouth with the back of his hand before taking a gulp of wine chilled with ice. "This was my father's place. I wandered around for years and years, working in the cotton gins, harvesting, whatever I could find. Going from one place to another. Must have been about ten years ago I settled down here for good."

"It's a lonely sort of place."

"I don't mind being alone. Anyway, now I've got Tapioca for company, haven't I, kid?"

"Have you been working with Mr. Brauer for long?"

Tapioca shrugged his shoulders and wiped his plate with a piece of bread, leaving it spotlessly clean.

"My assistant's a bit shy," said the Gringo. "Until he gets to know people, eh, kid?"

The mechanic finished eating, crossed his knife and fork, and leaned back in his chair with his hands on his swollen abdomen.

"And what about you? You said you were heading for Castelli?"

"Yes. We're going to see Pastor Zack. Do you know him?"

"Zack. Don't think so." The Gringo lit a cigarette. "I knew a Zack, when I was a kid, working at Pampa del Infierno. But he was no man of God, that guy. A Russian, a rough sort. A fighter. Always getting into trouble. There are lots of evangelists around here."

"Yes, there are many Protestant churches in the area. Ours has grown considerably over the last few years, thanks be to God. Pastor Zack has done wonderful work."

They sat there in silence. Brauer finished his wine and swirled the last little pieces of ice around in the bottom of the glass.

"Even if he doesn't believe, your friend, the one you were

talking about, he too can enter the Kingdom of Heaven. We all can," said the Reverend.

"What's it like?" asked Tapioca, avoiding the Reverend's eye. "The Kingdom of Heaven?"

"Come here, I will show you the bride, the wife of the Lamb," said Leni, butting in. They all looked at her: she had barely said a word since getting out of the car. "And he carried me away in the Spirit to a great and high mountain, and showed me the holy city, Jerusalem, coming down out of heaven from God, having the glory of God. Her brilliance was like a very costly stone, as a stone of crystal-clear jasper. It had a great and high wall. The material of the wall was jasper; and the city was pure gold. The foundation stones of the city wall were adorned with every kind of precious stone. The street of the city was pure gold, like transparent glass. Then the angel showed me a river of the water of life, clear as crystal, coming from the throne of God and of the Lamb, in the middle of its street. On either side of the river were the trees of life, yielding their fruit every month; and the leaves of the trees were for the healing of the nations." She smiled. "That's how it goes, isn't it, Father?"

"Is that all true?" asked Tapioca, astonished by the description.

"Of course not. It's metaphorical," Leni replied with a sneer.

"Elena," said the Reverend severely. "The Kingdom of Heaven is the most beautiful place you can imagine, son. Standing in the grace of God. All the treasures in the world put together couldn't compare with that. Are you a believer, Mr. Brauer?"

The Gringo poured himself some more wine and lit another cigarette.

"I don't have time for that stuff."

The Reverend smiled and held his gaze.

"Well, I don't have time for anything else."

"To each his own," said Brauer, getting up. "Clear the table, kid." Tapioca was sitting there lost in thought, rolling little pellets of bread and arranging them in a row.

The boy had arrived with his mother, one afternoon. He would have been about eight. They came in a truck that had picked them up in Sáenz Peña. The driver, who was heading to Rosario, filled up with gas, checked the tire pressure, and ordered a beer. While he was drinking it in the shade of the awning and the boy was playing with the dogs, the woman came over to Brauer, who was cleaning the spark plugs of a car that he had to repair. When he saw her approaching, he thought she must be looking for the bathroom; he had barely noticed her until then.

But it wasn't the bathroom she was after, it was something else.

"I want to talk with you."

Brauer glanced at her and went on with his work. She was hesitating; he thought she must be a prostitute. It wasn't unusual for long-haul truckers to take them from one place to another, and wait around while they turned a trick. Maybe they split the money after.

She was hesitating, so the Gringo said: "I'm listening."

"You don't remember me, do you?"

Brauer looked at her more carefully. No, he didn't remember her.

"It doesn't matter," she said. "We knew each other a long time ago, and not for long. Thing is, that's your son."

The Gringo put the spark plugs in a jar and wiped his hands on a rag. He looked to where she had pointed.

The boy was holding a branch. He was using it to play tug-of-war with one of the dogs; the others were circling him and jumping, impatient for their turn to play.

"They don't bite, do they?" she asked, anxiously.

"No, they don't bite," Brauer replied.

"Thing is, I can't go on raising him. I'm going to Rosario to look for work; it's harder with the kid. I still don't know where I'll end up. There's no one I can leave him with."

The Gringo finished wiping his hands and tucked the rag into his belt. He lit a cigarette and offered one to the woman.

"I'm Perico's sister. You worked with him at the Dobronich cotton gin in Machagai, if you remember."

"Perico. What's he up to?"

"Haven't heard from him in years. He went to Santiago, to work, and never came back."

The boy was lying on the ground and the dogs were snuffling at his ribs, looking for the stick hidden under his body. He was laughing like crazy.

"He's a good little kid," said the woman.

"How old is he?"

"Almost nine. He does what he's told and he's healthy. He's well brought up."

"Did he bring clothes?"

"There's a bag in the truck."

"All right. Leave him then," he said and flicked the cigarette butt away.

The woman nodded.

"His name is José Emilio, but everyone calls him Tapioca."

When the truck pulled away and began to climb slowly toward the road, Tapioca started crying. Standing still, he opened his mouth and let out a howl, and the tears ran down his dirty cheeks, leaving tracks. Brauer bent down to his level.

"Come on, kid, let's have a Coke and give those dogs something to eat."

Tapioca nodded, still watching the truck, which had climbed right up onto the road now, with his mother inside, taking her away forever.

Brauer picked up the bag and started walking toward the pump. The dogs had run up onto the verge, following the truck; now they were coming back with their tongues hanging out. The boy sniffled, turned around, and ran after the Gringo.

Tapioca started clearing the table and Leni got up to help him.

"Let me do it," she said, taking the knives and forks he was holding, then briskly gathering the plates and glasses. "Tell me where I can wash them."

"Over here."

Leni followed him to the back of the little house, where there was a cement tub with a faucet. As she washed up, she handed the things to Tapioca. The wet tableware piled up in his arms.

"Do you have a dishcloth?"

"Inside."

They went into the single room. It took Leni's eyes a few minutes to adjust to the darkness. Gradually she identified the shapes: a stove with a gas cylinder, a fridge, a small table, a few shelves nailed onto the wall, two folding beds, and a wardrobe. The bare cement floor was clean.

Tapioca put the things on the table and picked up a rag. Leni took it from him and started drying.

"You know where things go; you put them away," she said.

They finished the job in silence. When she had dried the last fork, Leni shook out the rag and hung it over the edge of the table.

"Done," she said with a satisfied smile.

Tapioca wiped his hands on the legs of his trousers, ill at ease.

Leni hardly ever did housework because she and her father

didn't have a home. Her clothes were sent to the laundry; they ate in dining rooms where other people cleared the table and washed the dishes; and the hotel beds they slept in were made and changed by the staff. So she took a certain pleasure in these tasks that another girl might have found tiresome. It was like playing house.

"What now?" she asked.

Tapioca shrugged.

"Let's go out," she said.

When they stepped outside, Leni's eyes had to adjust again, now to the fierce early-afternoon glare.

The Reverend was dozing on his chair, and Leni put a finger to her lips, warning Tapioca not to wake him. She walked away from the porch and beckoned to the boy, who followed her.

"Let's go under that tree," she said.

Tapioca tagged along. Except as a child, with his mother, he had never been in female company. Another boy would have resisted, feeling that the girl was pushing him around.

They sat down under the leafiest tree they could find. Even so, the hot wind smothered everything in a hellish torpor.

"Do you like music?" asked Leni.

Tapioca shrugged. Not that he disliked it. But he wasn't sure if he *liked* it, exactly. The radio was always on, and sometimes, when they played one of those cheerful, up-tempo *chamamés*, the Gringo would turn the volume right up. He'd always give a whoop and sometimes even dance a few steps, which amused Tapioca. Now that he thought about it, he liked the other kind more, the sad ones, about ghosts and tragic love affairs. *That* music was really beautiful; it made your heart go tight. It didn't make you want to dance; it made you want to keep still, watching the road.

"Put this in," said Leni, helping him to insert one of the little earphones. Then she put the other one into her ear. Tapioca looked at her. The girl smiled and pressed a button. At first, the music startled him: he'd never heard it so close up, as if it were playing in his brain. She shut her eyes; he did the same. Soon he got used to the melody, and it didn't feel like something that had intruded from outside. It was as if the music came surging up from his core.

6

The car had broken down as they were leaving Gato Colorado. Leni was amused by the name, and especially by the two cement cats, painted bright red, sitting on two pillars at the entrance to the town, which was on the border between the provinces of Santa Fe and Chaco.

The bad noises had begun much earlier, as they were coming in to Tostado, where they had spent the night in a small hotel. Leni said they should get it checked before setting off again, but the Reverend paid no attention.

"The car won't let us down. The good Lord wouldn't allow it."

Leni, who had been driving since she was ten and took turns at the wheel with her father, knew when a noise was just a noise and when it was a warning signal.

"We better get a mechanic to take a look before we leave," she insisted as they drank coffee early that morning in a bar. "We could ask here if they know someone who's good and doesn't charge too much."

"If we take it to a garage, they'll make us wait the whole day. We have to have faith. When has this car ever broken down, eh?"

Leni kept quiet. They always ended up doing what her father wanted, or, as he saw it, what God expected of them.

When they'd been on the road for two hours, the car gave one last snort and stopped. The Reverend tried to start it again, but it was no use. Leni looked through the bug-spotted windshield at the road stretching away and said, without turning, but in a clear and firm voice:

"I told you so, Father."

Pearson got out of the car, took off his jacket, and put it on the back of the seat. He shut the door, rolled up his sleeves, went around to the front, and opened the hood. A jet of smoke made him cough.

All Leni could see now was the hood with its chrome plating and smoke or steam coming out the sides. Then her father walked past; she heard him open the trunk and shift the suitcases. Two big, battered suitcases, secured with leather straps, which held all their belongings. In his: six shirts, three suits, an overcoat, undershirts, socks, underwear, another pair of shoes. In hers: three shirts, three skirts, two dresses, a coat, underwear, another pair of shoes. The Reverend slammed the trunk shut again.

Leni got out. The sun was scorching, and it was only nine in the morning. She undid the top two buttons of her shirt, walked around the car, and found her father putting down the triangles. She looked at the triangles and the deserted road. Between Tostado and where they were, they hadn't seen a single car.

"Any moment now a Good Samaritan will come along," said the Reverend, with his hands on his hips and a smile on his face, oozing faith.

She looked at him.

"The good Lord won't leave us stranded here," he said, rubbing his lower back, ruined by all those years of driving.

Leni thought that if one fine day the good Lord actually came down from the Kingdom of Heaven to attend to the Reverend's mechanical mishaps, her father would be more stunned than anyone. He'd fall on his ass. And piss himself too.

She took a few steps on the road, which was full of cracks and potholes. Her heels clicked on the concrete.

It was a place that seemed to have been completely forsaken by humans. Her gaze ranged over the stunted, dry, twisted trees and the bristly grass in the fields. From the very first day of Creation, God too had forsaken that place. But she was used to it. She'd spent her whole life in places like that.

"Don't go far," her father called out.

Leni lifted an arm to indicate that she had heard him.

"And get off the road; if someone comes, there could be an accident."

Leni laughed to herself. Yeah, or a hare might run her down. She turned her Walkman on and tried to find a station. Nothing. Only aimless static on the air. Steady white noise.

After a while she came back and leaned on the trunk, beside her father.

"Get in the car. This sun is fierce," said the Reverend.

"I'm fine."

She glanced across at him. He looked a bit downhearted.

"Someone will come, Father."

"Yes, of course. We must have faith. It's not a very busy road."

"I don't know. I saw a pair of guinea pigs up there. They went flying over the asphalt so they wouldn't burn their paws." Leni laughed, and so did the Reverend.

"Ah, my girl. Jesus has blessed me," he said, and tapped her on the cheek.

This meant that he was very glad to have her with him, thought Leni, but he could never say it like that, straight out: he always had to get Jesus in there, between them. At another moment, that display of diluted affection would have irritated her; but her father seemed vulnerable now, and she felt a little sorry for him. She knew that although he wouldn't admit it, he was ashamed of having ignored her advice. He was like a child who has messed up.

"How did it go again, that little verse about the Devil at siesta time?"

"What? A Bible verse?"

"No, just a verse, a little poem. What was it? Wait. It was funny."

"Elena, you shouldn't speak lightly of the Devil."

"Shhh. Wait, it's on the tip of my tongue. Okay, here we go. 'Setting his traps / he's gonna catch you / casting his line / he's gonna hook you / loading his gun / he's gonna hunt you / it's Satan, it's Satan, it's Satan.'"

Leni burst out laughing.

"There's more, but I forget."

"Elena, you turn everything into a joke. But the Devil is no laughing matter."

"It's just a *song*."

"Not one I know."

"But I used to sing it all the time when I was little."

"That's enough, Elena. You'll make up anything to torment me."

Leni shook her head. She wasn't making it up. That song existed. Of course it did. Then, suddenly, she remembered: she was sitting in the back seat of the car with her mother, in the parking lot of a service station; they were reciting the song and tapping their palms together like playmates, having some fun while the Reverend was in the bathroom.

"Look. There. Praise be to God," cried the Reverend and took two strides to the middle of the road, where he stood waving his arms at the bright, glinting point approaching quickly through the heat haze rising off the boiling asphalt.

The truck braked and pulled up sharply beside the Reverend. It was red, with a chrome bumper and tinted windows.

The driver lowered the window on the passenger side and the sound of the cassette player burst out like an explosion; the shock wave of a cumbia forced the Reverend to take a step back. The man leaned out and smiled and said something they couldn't hear. He disappeared back into the cool cabin, hit a button, and the music stopped. Then he reappeared. He was wearing reflective sunglasses; his skin was tanned, and he hadn't shaved for a few days.

"What's up, bud?"

The Reverend rested his hands on the window and leaned in to reply, still dazed by the music.

"Our car broke down."

The man got out the other side. The work clothes he was wearing contrasted with the sparkling, brand-new vehicle. He approached the car and had a look under the hood, which was still propped open.

"If you like, I can tow you to the Gringo's place."

"We're not from around here."

"Gringo Brauer has a garage a few miles away. He'll be able to fix it for sure. I'd take you into town, but on a Saturday, with this heat, it'd be hard to find anyone who could help you. They've all gone to Paso de la Patria or the Bermejito to cool off a bit. Me too: I'm going home to get my reel, pick up a few pals, and good luck to anyone who wants me before Monday."

The man laughed.

"Well, if you don't mind."

"Of course not, bud. I'm not going to leave you out here in the middle of nowhere, on foot. Not even the spirits are out in this heat."

He climbed back into his truck and drove it to the front of

the car. Then he got out, took a steel cable from the back, and attached the car's bumper to his tow bar.

"Let's go, bud. In you get; it's good and cool with the air-con."

The Reverend sat in the middle; Leni sat next to the door. Everything smelled of leather and those little perfumed pine trees.

"Passing through?" asked the driver.

"We're going to see an old friend," said the Reverend.

"Well, then, welcome to hell."

7

Leni's last image of her mother is from the rear window of the car. Leni is inside, kneeling on the seat, with her arms and chin on the top of the backrest. Outside, her father has just slammed the trunk shut, after taking out a suitcase and putting it on the ground beside her mother, who is standing there with her arms crossed, wearing the sort of long skirt that Leni wears now. Behind them, over the dirt road of that anonymous town, a backdrop of dawn sky rises, pink and gray. Leni is sleepy; her mouth feels sticky and tastes of toothpaste—they left the hotel without having breakfast.

Her mother uncrosses her arms and wipes her forehead with one hand. The Reverend is speaking to her, but from the car Leni can't hear what he's saying. He's moving his hands a lot. He raises an index finger, lowers it and points at her mother, shakes his head, and keeps talking softly. The way his mouth is moving, it's like he's biting each word before he spits it out.

Her mother starts walking toward the car, but the Reverend blocks her way, and she freezes. Like in statues, thinks Leni, who has played that game so often, in so many different yards, with different children every time, after the Sunday sermon. With one arm extended, palm out, the Reverend, her father, walks backward and opens the driver's door. Her mother is left standing there, beside the suitcase. She covers her face with her hands. She's crying.

The car starts and pulls away, raising a cloud of dust. Her mother runs after it for a few yards, like a dog dumped beside the road at the beginning of a vacation.

This happened almost ten years ago. The details of her mother's face have faded from Leni's memory, but not the shape of her body—tall, slim, elegant. When she looks at herself in the mirror, she feels that she has inherited her bearing. At first she thought it was just wishful thinking, wanting to resemble her. But since becoming a woman, she has caught her father, more than once, looking at her with a blend of fascination and contempt, the way you might look at someone who stirs up a mixture of good and bad memories.

The Reverend and Leni have never spoken of that episode. She doesn't know the name of the town where they left her mother, although if they went back to that street, she's sure she would recognize it immediately. Places like that don't change much over the years. The Reverend, of course, must remember the exact point on the map where he left his wife, and must, of course, have struck it off his itinerary for good.

From that morning on, Reverend Pearson has presented himself as a widowed pastor with a young girl in his care. A man in such circumstances elicits instant trust and sympathy. If his wife has been snatched away by God in the prime of life, leaving him alone with a little girl, and he carries on, firm in his faith, burning with the flame of Christ's love, he must be a good man, a man who deserves to be listened to attentively.

Tapioca's memories of his mother are vague too. After she left him, he had to get used to his new home. What interested him most was the heap of old cars. The dogs and that mechanical cemetery were a comfort in the first weeks while he was still adjusting. He would spend all day among the car bodies: he played at driving them, with three or four dogs as copilots. The Gringo left him to it and approached the boy gradually, as if taming a wild animal. He began by telling him the stories of all those cars and the streets and roads they had traveled. Many had gone to faraway places: not just Rosario, like Tapioca's mother, but Buenos Aires and Patagonia. Brauer dug out a pile of Automobile Club road maps, and at night, after dinner, he showed the boy the places where, according to him, those cars had been. He traced the routes with his thick finger, stained with grease and nicotine, and explained that the breadth and color of the lines on the map showed how important the various roads were. Sometimes Brauer's finger changed direction abruptly, turning off the main highway to follow a barely hinted at track, a line finer than an eyelash, ending in a tiny dot. That, the Gringo would say, was where the driver of the car had spent the night, and the time had come for them to go to sleep as well.

Sometimes the mechanic's fingertip skipped along a dotted line, a bridge built over a river. Tapioca didn't understand about rivers or bridges, so Brauer explained.

Sometimes his finger moved slowly around the curves of a mountain road. Once it came to the edge of the map, and the Gringo spoke of the cold, a cold they would never know in Chaco, a cold that made everything white. The highway was covered with ice there in winter, and the ice made tires skid and caused fatal accidents. The thought of a place like that scared Tapioca, and he was glad they were high up on the map and not down there at the end of the world.

Gringo Brauer bought the cars from the provincial police. He had a contact. They sold them to him for scrap. Mainly they were cars impounded after accidents or fires. Every now and then they'd get a stolen one. The Gringo would check the mechanics; the police would supply new papers and license plates, and the car would be sold to the Gypsies. The police paid Brauer for the work, with a bonus for his cooperation.

Along with the stories about where the cars had been, the Gringo would tell Tapioca about how they had changed hands and ended up there at the garage. He re-created accidents, and Tapioca listened with wide-open eyes. In the first stories, the driver and passengers would climb out unharmed; the car was a write-off but the people were safe and sound. After a while, the Gringo thought it was time to get the boy used to death, and from then on all the endings were definitive and bloody. This gave Tapioca nightmares for a while. He saw his mother or Brauer himself or the few people he knew dying in wrecks of twisted metal, their bodies flying through the windshield or burnt to a cinder when the car burst into flames and they were trapped by doors that wouldn't open. But eventually he got used to it and stopped dreaming about the scenes that the Gringo had described.

It's not the cars' fault, Brauer always told him. It's the people who drive them.

Tapioca was in third grade when his mother left him. He could read, write, and do sums. The Gringo hadn't finished school himself, so he didn't see why the boy had to keep on with it. The nearest school was miles away, and it would have been complicated to take him there and fetch him every day. The formal schooling he'd received up to the age of eight was enough. From then on, Brauer decided, Tapioca would have to learn by working and observing nature. It might not be scientific, but nature and work would teach the kid how to be a good person.

God has given us words. Words set us apart from all the other crea-
tures living under this sky. But beware of words, for they are weap-
ons that may be wielded by the Devil.

How often have you said: What a good speaker this man is,
what beautiful words, such a rich vocabulary; listening to him is so
reassuring.

The boss comes and speaks to you with strong, dependable words,
making promises for the long term. He speaks like a father to his chil-
dren. After hearing him, you say to each other: How well he spoke; his
words are simple and true; he speaks to us as if we were his children; he
made it clear that if we stay with him and do as he says, he will always
keep us safe from harm, like members of his family; he will never fail us;
he said it plain as day, with simple words; he spoke to us as an equal.

The politician comes and speaks to you with fine-sounding words,
as if there were music coming out of his mouth; no one has ever spoken
to you with such beautiful words, so fluently, without ever running
out of breath. And after such a flowery speech, so carefully written, so
correct, with so many words from the dictionary, you are meek and
docile. You go away thinking: He really is a good man; he's thinking
for all of us; he thinks what we think; he's representing us.

But I say to you: Beware of strong words and beautiful words.
Beware of the boss's words and the words of the politician. Beware of
those who say they are your father or your friend. Beware of these men
who speak on their own behalf to further their own interests.

You already have a father, and that father is God. You already have a friend, and that friend is Christ. All the rest is words. Words that blow away in the wind.

You have your own words, the power of the word, and you must use that power. God doesn't listen to the loudest or the most eloquent speakers; he listens to those who speak truthfully, from the heart.

Let Christ speak through your mouths, let your tongues move to the rhythm of his word: the one true word. Take up the weapon of the word and aim; fire at the charlatans, the liars, the false prophets.

Open yourselves to the word of God; let it rule, for it is powerful and alive and sharper than any double-edged sword, and it plunges deep into the soul and the spirit, into the joints and the marrow, and finds out the thoughts and intentions of the heart.

Consider this and testify.

Praised be the word of the Father and the Son.

8

Tapioca removed the earphone and stood up slowly so as not to wake the girl. He took a few steps and shook the dirt off his trousers. Then he headed for the bathroom. He tiptoed past the Reverend, who was still dozing on his chair.

Tapioca emptied his bladder noisily into the toilet. Just as well the girl, Leni, was out of earshot, otherwise he would have been embarrassed.

When he came out again, drying his hands on the front of his shirt, the Reverend was waking up. He had taken off his glasses and was using his handkerchief to wipe his sweaty face and his scalp, with its few remaining strands of hair. He saw Tapioca and smiled.

"Take a seat, my boy."

He patted the chair beside him. Tapioca looked at him with his head tilted to one side, like a dog that has been called. The stranger was making him nervous, and he hesitated for a while, trying to think of an excuse to get away. But in the end he sat down.

"They call you Tapioca, don't they?"

He nodded.

"What's your name?"

"Tapioca."

"That's what they call you. It's your nickname. But you have another name, the one you were given when you were born. Do you remember what it is?"

Tapioca rubbed his hands on his trousers.

"Josemilio," he blurted.

"José. That's a nice name. A very fine name. Do you know who José is?"

Brushing away a fly that was crawling on his face, Tapioca looked at the Reverend. This man was confusing him. He shrugged in reply.

"José was María's husband, María, the mother of Christ. José was the man who raised him, like Mr. Brauer. He raised you as if you were his son, didn't he? Do you know who Christ is?"

The boy wiped his face with his hand. He was sweating. It wasn't so much because of the heat (he was used to that); it was nerves. He wanted to get away. But he was intimidated by the stranger.

"Have you heard of God? God is our creator. He created everything you can see. You are his work and so am I. Mr. Brauer has told you about God, hasn't he?"

Tapioca looked at him. He remembered the years when he went to school, when the teacher asked him questions, and he didn't know the answer. It was like that now; he felt like crying.

"I have to take something to the Gringo," he stammered.

"Wait. You can go in a minute," said the Reverend, placing his hand on the boy's arm. It was as soft as a woman's hand. Although it was warm, it made Tapioca shiver.

He looked to see where Brauer was. The Gringo was bent over with his head under the hood of the Reverend's car, more than a hundred yards from the porch where Tapioca was being detained, and completely unaware of his distress.

"Don't worry. I'll tell him we were having a chat."

The man looked at him with a calm smile. It wasn't the first time Tapioca had seen such light eyes; there were lots of gringos in the area. But these eyes seemed to be casting a spell on him. It was like what Brauer had said about the pygmy owl and its prey: the gaze of the owl was so powerful that its victims would faint before they were eaten.

Tapioca shook his head. It felt heavy. He didn't have to look into those eyes.

"Hmm?" said the Reverend's honey-sweet voice.

"What?" said the boy, almost irritably.

"So no one ever told you about Christ our Savior. Mr. Brauer is a good man. And you're a good boy, José. Christ is waiting for you with open arms. We just have to prepare you to welcome him."

I don't know what you're talking about. Christ and all that stuff. You come here and you start talking to me. My . . . my name is Tapioca, okay? You don't know the first thing about us.

He would have liked to say something like that to end the conversation. But he didn't dare; he sat there with his mouth shut. He looked all around to avoid looking at the Reverend, but his eyes couldn't settle anywhere: they jumped from one of the dogs to the road, and then to the cars piled up in the sun, back to the tip of his sandals, to his hands, and finally stole a sidelong glance at the man sitting beside him.

The Reverend's gaze, by contrast, was fixed on the boy. He was sitting now with hands clasped, in a beatific pose.

"It isn't enough to be good in this world, José. We have to use our goodness to serve Christ. Only he can keep us from evil. If we welcome Christ into our hearts, we will never be alone again. Maybe you don't know this because nobody has told you yet, but dark days are coming . . . bad days, I mean, terrible days, like you can't imagine. Although Christ's power is infinite, the Devil is very strong too. Not as strong as Jesus, praise him . . . but the Devil does battle day and night. That's why we have to join Christ's ranks, José. To build up a big, strong army, to banish the Devil from this world for good. The final war is coming, José. On the day when the archangels sound their clarions, only those who have given themselves to Christ will be able to hear. On the Day of Judgment, those who hear the clarions will be saved; they will enter the Kingdom of Heaven."

Tapioca listened attentively. His eyes had stopped trying to slip away from the Reverend's gaze; they were fixed on him now. He was still afraid. But not of the Reverend, who was coming to seem like a friend or something more: a father, a guide. He was afraid of what the Reverend was talking about. He was afraid of not being ready when all those terrible things began to happen. The Gringo can't have known about it, or he would have told him already. Up to that moment, Brauer had been the wisest person Tapioca knew. But there was clearly a limit to the wisdom of his boss.

"And the Gringo?" he asked.

"What will happen to Mr. Brauer?"

"Is he going to go with us, where you said, to heaven?"

"Of course. Mr. Brauer will enter the Kingdom of the Just along with you, José. If you join Christ's Army, you'll be able to take along all the people in your heart. Mr. Brauer looked after you when you were a child and you couldn't take care of yourself. He fed you, he cared for you when you were sick, he taught you lots of things, didn't he?"

Tapioca nodded.

"Good. Now you're the one who's going to look after him and show him how to love Jesus. That's the most beautiful gift you can give Mr. Brauer."

Tapioca smiled. The fear was still there like a weasel in its burrow; he could see the little eyes shining in the darkness. But he was also beginning to feel something new, a kind of fire in his gut that was filling him with courage. And yet something was still bothering him.

"And the dogs? Can I take them too?"

Pearson almost laughed, but he controlled himself.

"Of course. The Kingdom of Heaven is a big place, and Christ loves animals. The dogs can come too. Of course! Why not?"

The Reverend opened his mouth and breathed in. His mouth was dry.

"Could you bring me a glass of water, José?"

Sometimes, much to his regret, he felt that it was hopeless, that whatever he did, he and others like him, they would always arrive too late: the Devil was always a step ahead. A step ahead of Christ himself, he sometimes thought, God forgive him. Finding a boy like Tapioca filled him with faith and hope. A pure soul. Still a little rough around the edges, admittedly, but that's what the Reverend was there for. He would sculpt that soul with Christ's chisels and turn it into a beautiful work to offer up to God.

Thinking about it gave him strength and reaffirmed his purpose. Once again, he felt that he was an arrow burning with the flame of Christ. And the bow that is drawn to shoot that arrow as far as possible, straight to the spot where the flame will ignite a raging fire. And the wind that spreads the fire that will lay waste to the world with the love of Jesus.

9

Drinking the water, the Reverend remembered going down the bluff as a child, holding his mother's hand. She strode ahead, pulling hard on his little arm. The slope was steep and he had to dig his heels in among the weed-covered clods to stop himself from falling. They were both out of breath from the walk.

His mother's skirt moved in front of him like a curtain revealing and hiding the landscape as the cloth blew about in the wind.

He didn't know where they were going, but before they set out, his mother had told him that it would be a day to remember. She dressed him in his best clothes and took care with hers as well. They left the house after lunch and took the bus to the center of town. There they caught another bus with a sign on the front saying *Beach*. They were the only passengers who went all the way to the end. The driver switched off the engine on a dirt road at the top of the bluff and pointed the way down to the shore.

What looked like a dark blotch from up there, or perhaps an uneven patch of ground, turned out to be, as they came closer, a small multitude. A hundred people standing, facing the river, and singing. Now that they were almost down on the beach, they could hear the song, carried by the wind. It wasn't a song the child had heard before, on the radio or anywhere else. It seemed fairly cheerful, but as they approached, a feeling of deep sadness overtook him. Perhaps because of the overcast sky, and the trash that people had dropped and the river had gathered and dumped on that beach, where the local authorities left it to rot. Perhaps he had hoped that his mother was taking him somewhere else, to the movies or an amusement park.

They stopped to catch their breath, and his mother let go of his hand to tidy up her bun. Then she combed his hair with her fingers, smoothed down his clothes, and tied one of his shoelaces.

"Come on," she said, and took his hand again. She pushed her way through the crowd. People frowned at her while continuing to sing, but she kept going as if she hadn't noticed. She moved her mouth as if singing or apologizing, although she was doing neither.

They made their way to the front row, where the beach was mud and slime. He could feel his shoes sinking into the sogginess. His best shoes. He looked anxiously at his mother. But she was ignoring him. Like the others, she was watching the dark river ruffled by the wind.

Why were they there with that bunch of singing weirdos, instead of on the square, dipping their fingers in cotton candy, filling their mouths with sickly sweet foam?

What was so interesting about all that water?

Then the unexpected happened. The song stopped. A man's head emerged, long hair plastered to his skull. He broke the surface of the river and rose up, torso bare and arms outstretched. He began to walk toward the shore, a gentle wake lapping about his ankles.

Someone, a man or a woman, the boy couldn't tell, began to chant in the most beautiful voice he had ever heard.

Without a second thought, his mother grabbed him under the arms and threw him to the river man, who caught him in an icy, wet embrace.

Whenever he remembers that day, which was to determine the rest of his life, the Reverend is overcome by emotion. Whenever he feels himself weakening, he summons that memory: the day of his baptism, the afternoon when the river man plunged him in the filthy waters of the Paraná to lift him out again, purified, and give him back into God's care. Thinking about it strengthens him, reaffirms his sense of mission.

He once asked his mother why she had taken him to the river that afternoon. She had never been a believer.

"I just thought I would," she told him. "I heard on the radio that the Preacher was coming, and I thought I'd go and see what it was about. Just out of curiosity. There'd been so much talk about him, all week. I don't know why I thought he could help us. And when I got there and saw all those people, I thought: We have to be in the front row." His mother laughed as if remembering a prank. "And when we were in the front row, I thought: He has to hold the boy. I knew that if the Preacher took you in his arms, if I could just get his attention, something good was bound to come of it."

His mother bent over her needlework again. That was when he was twenty years old and starting to build up a reputation. She no longer had to work to pay the bills. A few years earlier they had left Paraná and gone to live in Rosario, where they were fed and housed by the church. Her son was a young pastor with a bright future. All through the region people were starting to recognize his talent for preaching.

She went on doing embroidery because it was something she enjoyed, and out of habit, to keep herself busy. Even when the

Preacher had taken them in and given them his protection, she showed no interest in religion. For her, it was as if her son had become a doctor or a lawyer. As if she had given him a university education, or set him up in a profession that provided a decent living.

He was grateful to his mother for having thrown him into the Preacher's arms, and into the new life that was opening before him. But deep down he found her indifference galling.

Every time he came down from the pulpit, she was the first to rush up and hug him.

"You really knocked them out," she would say with a wink.

She thought he was putting it on; she regarded her son as a consummate con man: thanks to his rare gift for eloquence, they would always have food on the table and a roof over their heads.

And she was not the only one who had a stake in his gift. His superiors, even the Preacher himself—he soon came to realize—also believed that they had found the goose that laid the golden eggs. With every word that came out of his mouth, coins rained into the coffers of the temple.

"You have surpassed your master," the Preacher used to say to him.

By then, the thin man with feverish eyes who had risen from the river was long gone. He had grown fat and lost his hair; he no longer stood in the mud; and it had been many years since he had plunged faithless bodies into the water and lifted them out again, unharmed, their lungs pumped full of Christ's glory.

Give your best to God: that was the sentence he heard, repeated like a psalm, as the assistants moved among the faithful, holding tins for the collection. Give your best to God, and the coins poured down like a rain of toads. Give your best to God, and the notes glided silently into the tins.

Give your best to God and *You really knocked them out* resounded in his head as he tried to recover, sweaty and still buzzing, in a corner of the temple.

He couldn't tell his mother how uncomfortable he felt, since she had been the first to misinterpret his intentions. So when she died, not long after the conversation about his baptism, he felt a great relief, God forgive him.

His mother left this world content. Although her life had been full of frustrations—scared that she would be left on the shelf, she had yielded to the charms of an American adventurer and married him only to be abandoned while she was still pregnant—her son at least was in clover, as she liked to say, congratulating herself on having secured his future, thanks to the brilliant idea that had come to her one fine day as she sat peering at her needlework and listening to the radio.

Pearson fervently believed in every word that came out of his mouth. He believed because those words were grounded in Jesus Christ. He was the doll through which the great ventriloquist of the universe spoke.

It never mattered to the Reverend whether his stage was in a city temple—an old cinema, for example, with boxes, re-upholstered seats, a carpeted floor, and a red curtain that opened only when he was in place behind it—or a storehouse with whitewashed walls to keep the vermin out, a tin roof, and folding wooden chairs bought at a farm clearance sale. Given a choice, he always preferred a simple venue, without any special facilities: no air-conditioning, no sound system, no blinding lights.

He rarely visited the big cities. He preferred the dusty roads abandoned by the Highway Authority, and the people abandoned by the government, like the recovered alcoholics who, thanks to the word of Christ, had become pastors in small communities:

men who worked in construction, and went door to door in the evenings selling Bibles and religious magazines, and stood up on Sundays at the front of the hall, without the strength that drink used to give them, and spoke, with a certain awkwardness, perhaps, but fueled and sustained by Christ.

10

Leni woke up dazed. It took her a moment to remember where she was, and how she had ended up under that tree. She was all sweaty, and her body was stiff from sitting on the hard ground and leaning against that rough trunk. Like a cat, she wiped her face with her hands to remove the sleep from her eyes, and yawned. She saw her father on the porch, talking with Tapioca. She smiled. Reverend Pearson wouldn't give up until he had converted that boy.

She turned her head. Off in the distance, oblivious to his customer's evangelical designs, Gringo Brauer was working on the car.

Leni had conflicting feelings: she admired the Reverend deeply but disapproved of almost everything her father did. As if he were two different people. Earlier, she had told him to leave Tapioca alone, but if she had joined them on the porch now, she too would have been captivated by his words.

Before the Reverend walks onto the stage to deliver a sermon, Leni always shines his shoes until they gleam. She brushes his suit, adjusts his black silk tie and the white handkerchief that peeps from his breast pocket like the ears of a little rabbit. She takes his glasses and puts them away in the case. The Reverend never wears glasses when he is addressing a congregation. His face must be bare; nothing must come between his eyes and those of the faithful. Pale as a mountain river, those eyes are part of his magnetism. Eyes that in the course of a sermon can mist over, darken, or flicker and burn.

She takes a step back to check his overall appearance. If everything is in order, she smiles and gives him a thumbs-up.

Although she has seen it over and over, for as long as she can remember, every time the Reverend walks onstage, Leni feels the same vibration in her body. Something wonderful is happening. Something she can't explain in words.

Sometimes she can't help herself: she can't stay there in the wings, where she should be in case he needs her; she has to go and join the faithful.

She wonders if one day the Reverend will take her by the wrist and lead her up to the front, if he will bite her chest and tear out the black thing once and for all, the thing she can feel inside her at night, when she lies on the hotel bed, or during the day, in the car, when she's traveling with her father.

Leni stood up and lifted her arms, stretching them skyward to decompress her spine. Removing the barrette, she shook out her brown hair and combed it with her fingers, then drew it back into a ponytail. She took out the earphone and switched off the radio.

It had taken months to convince her father to buy her that little portable player. She promised him that she would listen to Christian music, nothing else, and she always kept a cassette in it, just in case. But the only time the little wheels turned was when her father remembered to check. She used the Walkman to listen to FM radio. Music programs with people writing or calling in to request songs and send messages. Once, for the worldly pleasure of being on the radio, she snuck away to a telephone booth and called in to one of those programs. They took her message and broadcast it. But it turned out that they didn't have her song. They apologized: Hey, sorry, Leni, we don't have it, but you're going to love this one. What they played was nothing like her request, but that didn't matter. The fun was in having called, and knowing that her name had traveled on the airwaves, within a four-mile radius of that local radio station, which no doubt operated out of somebody's kitchen.

She decided to go for a walk to blow away the cobwebs. She set off in the opposite direction from the little house and the pile of scrap metal.

The landscape was desolate: every so often a twisted black tree, with sparse leaves and a bird on a branch, so motionless it might have been stuffed.

She walked until she came to the edge of the property, marked by a sagging wire fence. Beyond was a cotton field. It wasn't yet harvest time, but the plants, with their rough, dark leaves, were showing their bolls. Some were already ripe and splitting, with bits of white fluff coming out. In a few weeks, the crop would be harvested and sent to the gins. There the fiber would be separated from the seed and packed into bales to be sold.

Leni touched her sweaty shirt. She remembered her father once saying that her grandmother had been an embroiderer. She had nimble fingers, he had said. A vaguely nostalgic thought crossed Leni's mind: the cloth her grandmother had embroidered and the shirt she was wearing now had both originated in the solitude of a cotton field like that.

11

"Where were you, kid?" asked Brauer, wiping his hands on a rag.

"Over there. Talking with the man."

"Since when are you such a big talker?"

Tapioca turned away and pursed his lips.

"You want to tell me what you were talking about?"

"Jesus Christ."

"Jesus Christ. How about that?"

"Yes, the man, he was telling me all this stuff I didn't know," Tapioca replied enthusiastically.

"About Jesus Christ?"

"And the end of the world. If you could see what it's going to be like . . ."

"And what's it going to be like?" asked the Gringo, taking a cigarette from the pack and putting it in his mouth.

"Terrible. Really terrible."

Tapioca shook his head as if trying to dislodge the dark thoughts that were filling it. Brauer lit his cigarette and blew out a jet of smoke.

The boy looked up, smiling.

"But we'll go to the Kingdom of Heaven because we're good."

"Ah, well, that's reassuring," said the Gringo ironically, although his assistant's religious fervor was beginning to disturb him.

"Us and the dogs. Because Christ likes dogs too. And . . . and . . ."

"That's enough, kid. Listen to me. We can talk about going to heaven later. You've got to help me here now. It's worse than I thought. Go and make some *maté* and bring it over. The man can entertain himself. I need you to come back and give me a hand, okay?"

Tapioca said yes, turned around, and headed for the house.

"Don't let the water boil and wash out my *maté*, eh?" the Gringo called after him.

He leaned against the car and finished his cigarette, inhaling deeply. He had no time for lofty thoughts. Religion was for women and the weak. Good and evil were everyday things, things in the world you could reach out and touch. Religion, in his view, was just a way of ignoring responsibilities. Hiding behind God, waiting to be saved, or blaming the Devil for the bad things you do.

He had taught Tapioca to respect the natural world. He believed in the forces of nature. But he had never mentioned God. He could see no reason to talk about something he thought irrelevant.

From time to time, they would go into the forest and observe its behavior. The forest: one great creature seething with life. A man could learn all he needed to know just by watching nature at work. Everything was written there in the forest, continually, as if in a book of inexhaustible wisdom. The mystery and its revelation. Everything, if you could learn to hear and see what nature had to tell and show.

They would keep still for hours, in among the trees, attuning their ears until they could tell a lizard crawling on a piece of bark from a worm wriggling on a leaf. You just had to listen to apprehend the pulse of the universe.

When he was younger, Tapioca had been scared of will-o'-the-wisps. One of the good-for-nothings who came to the garage told him a bunch of stories, and after that the kid was too scared to go out and piss on his own at night. He couldn't sleep and the next day he'd wander around like a zombie. One night, fed up with all that nonsense, the Gringo took him by the scruff of the neck and led him out into the fields. They wandered around for hours until at last, just before dawn, they found what the mechanic was looking for. Far off, among the trees, they saw a quivering brightness.

"There's your will-o'-the-wisp," he said.

The kid started bawling, and the Gringo had to take him by the arm and drag him to the site of the discovery.

Beneath the trees they found the carcass of a medium-sized animal: a goat or a small calf. Brauer pointed the flashlight to show Tapioca the little flames that were rising from the putrid flesh and fluttering in the dark night air.

Now he was thinking that perhaps he should have warned the kid about the stories in the Bible. It had been simple to find a natural explanation for the will-o'-the-wisp. It wouldn't be so easy to get that stuff about God out of his head.

12

"Excuse me," said the Reverend.

Brauer, who had gone back to work on the motor, started and bumped his head against the inside of the hood.

"I'm sorry. I didn't mean to frighten you. I'm just going to get some things out of the car."

"Feel free. It's yours," said the Gringo grumpily, rubbing his head with his fingers.

The Reverend leaned into the back of the car and reappeared with a pile of books.

"How's it going?"

"It's trickier than I thought. I'm trying to figure it out, but I don't know if I can fix it."

"Don't worry. We're not in a rush."

"I thought you were expected somewhere."

"They know we're coming in the next few days. But not exactly when. The ways of the Lord are mysterious; you never know what can happen, so I prefer not to be too precise about my arrival time, otherwise people get worried, you see."

"Sure. If I can't fix it, I'll take you to Du Gratty. You'll be able to find somewhere to spend the night there."

"Let's not get ahead of ourselves. There are still a few hours of daylight left, Mr. Brauer. You carry on; don't worry about us. We're happy to be here, my daughter and I, getting to know you and José. We've been on the road long enough to know that patience is a good counselor. There's a reason for every turn of events, even if we don't know what it is."

The Reverend walked away with his books. Brauer stood there watching him go back to the house and settle down again under the awning.

He shook his head. The sooner he could get that damned car fixed the better. He could already see himself giving the Reverend and his daughter the beds, while Tapioca and he slept on the floor along with the dogs.

Why hadn't he listened to Tapioca? They should have gone fishing that morning, like the kid wanted to. But he had said no: with the heat, the Bermejito would be packed; you could never catch anything there on the weekends; all those people made so much noise it scared the fish away.

Anyway. He too had learned that patience is a good counselor. With patience and saliva . . . he thought and bent over the motor again.

"Boss," cried Tapioca.

The Gringo raised his head suddenly and bumped it again in the same place.

"Jesus, kid, what is it?"

"Here's the *maté*."

"What the . . . why'd you have to yell out like that and make me jump? Can't you see I'm trying to concentrate here?"

"How am I supposed to know?"

"Blahblah . . . shut up and brew it. I don't know what's gotten into you today, you're chattering away like a parrot."

Tapioca laughed and handed him the *maté*.

"Careful, it's hot."

"Didn't I tell you to watch the kettle?"

"What can I do? It's like that when it comes out of the faucet. I didn't let it boil, but it's pretty hot."

"Right. You brew two *matés* like this, and then it's all washed out, and you're done. Clever, aren't you? Hand me that spanner. And brew me another one; it's not bad."

"I can make you a *tereré* if you like."

"That's for women, kid. You have to make *maté* with hot water. As my dad used to say: it warms you up in winter, and in summer it cools you down."

"Was he good, your father?"

"Good? I guess so. He didn't kill anyone, as far as I know."

"The man said I have the same name as Jesus's father."

"Was he called Tapioca?"

"José, Gringo. My name is José."

"I know, kid. I was joking."

"Except he wasn't the real father. But he brought him up. Like you brought me up."

"Here, take this and clean it for me."

"God is your father."

"Give me the *maté*."

"You're like my father, Gringo."

"Here."

"I'm never going to forget what you've done for me."

"Come over here. Hold these cables for me. Apart."

The body is Christ's temple. Each one of your bodies houses a soul, and within each soul dwells Christ the Lord. So the body cannot be bad.

Look at yourselves.

Each one of you is a unique and perfect creation. Each one has been imagined by the greatest artist of all time.

Praise be to God.

You might say to me: Reverend, I have only one leg, or one arm; I lost a hand in an accident; my spine is broken and I can't walk. You might say: Reverend, I am blind in one eye, I limp, I stutter, I have lost a breast, I have an extra finger. You might say: Reverend, I am old, I have lost my teeth and my hair, I am a human wreck. Reverend, I'm no use for anything, I'm ugly, I'm sick, I'm ashamed of my body. You can come to me dragging your torso without any legs to carry it. You can come to me completely paralyzed, with your mouth all twisted and drooling. You can come to me covered with sores and wounds, with scars all over your skin. You can come to me in the minute before death takes you and still I will say: You are beautiful because you are the work of God.

Praise be to the Lord.

I ask you then: If your body is the temple of Christ, why do you mistreat it? Why do you let yourselves be oppressed, violated, beaten? I ask the women: Why do you let your husbands or fiancés or fathers or brothers abuse your bodies? And the bodies of your children? How often have you justified a push, a slap, or an insult in the name of love? And I ask each man: How often have you used your body, the body that God has given you, the body that should be the temple of Christ and not the Devil's lair, how often have you used it to hurt other people?

If a group of men burst in here right now and started kicking things, breaking chairs, burning the curtains, would you all just sit there and do nothing to protect this place? I am sure that you would all rise up and use your strength to throw out the intruders; you would all defend this church that Christ inspired you to build with your own hands.

I ask you then: Why do you not defend your bodies in the same way?

If the healthiest person among you were to go out naked into the street on a rainy winter night, that person would have a ninety-nine percent chance of catching pneumonia. In just the same way, if you expose your body to sin, there is a ninety-nine percent chance that the Devil will take it.

Christ is love. But don't confuse love with passivity. Don't confuse love with cowardice. Don't confuse love with slavery. Christ's flame illuminates, but it can also light a raging fire.

Consider this and testify.

13

Brauer started the car and sat there listening, his head against the steering wheel. It was sounding better. He got out and bent over the motor, straining to hear. He smiled. He had finally narrowed it down.

He needed a bit of a rest. And something cold to drink.

As he approached the porch, the Reverend looked up from his books and smiled at him.

The Gringo waved and headed for the bathroom. After emptying his bladder, he took off his shirt. He turned on the faucet, put his head and torso under the shower, and waited for the water to cool down. He picked up a cake of soap and lathered his arms, his neck, his armpits, and his hair. And he leaned there, with his hands on the untiled wall, letting the soapy foam run off his body and gather around the sinkhole in the floor. He turned off the faucet and shook the water out of his hair, like a dog. He grabbed a towel that was hanging from a hook and dried himself. Then he put his shirt back on and went out again, refreshed.

The Reverend had gone back to his books. Brauer walked behind him, stepped inside, and came out with an ice-cold bottle of beer and two glasses. He stood beside the table. Pearson lifted his head and smiled at him again.

Brauer rested the bottle on his thigh and prized the top off with his lighter. He poured himself a glass.

"Would you like one?"

"No thank you. I don't drink."

"It's good and cold," said the Gringo, and took a very long gulp that left foam on his mustache. "Looks like I got a handle on your car."

"Is it ready?"

"Not yet. I don't want to get ahead of myself, but you should be good to go pretty soon."

"As I said, there's no hurry."

"But your friends are waiting for you, Reverend. You must be keen to see them."

"Pastor Zack and his family are always in my heart. I know I'll be hugging them soon; there's no reason to be impatient."

"Whatever you say. If I was you, I'd want to get there by dinnertime. It's nice to share a meal with old friends, don't you think?"

"With old friends. And with new friends. Yes, of course. Tell me, Brauer, I was wondering, is there a stream around here?"

"A stream? Fat chance. With this drought, there's not even a miserable water hole left. It's all gone; the earth has drunk it all. Haven't you seen the cracks? They're wider than my finger. You want to go fishing, do you?"

"You could say that. You know, I'm going to take you up on that glass of beer, a small one. Why not?"

Brauer poured him a glass and filled his own again. He pulled up a chair, sat down opposite Pearson (their knees almost touched under the table), and gave him a long, hard look. The Gringo's small blue eyes, reddened slightly by the glare and the drink, sought out the watery eyes of the Reverend.

"What are you after?" he asked.

Pearson took two little birdlike sips and smiled benevolently. "What do you mean?"

"Why were you putting ideas into Tapioca's head?"

The Reverend took off his glasses, folded them carefully, and slipped them into his shirt pocket.

"I wasn't putting anything into his head. I'd say I was speaking to his heart."

"Don't bullshit me, Pearson."

"I was talking with José about God. You've done a good job with that boy, Brauer; you've raised him on your own, as if he were your son. His heart is pure. I've been traveling around for many years now. I raised my daughter on my own too. And, believe me, that boy has a purity that is very hard to find. As I was saying, you've done a great job, but, if I may say so, his religious education has been rather neglected."

"Tapioca's a good kid, Pearson."

"Absolutely. I'm not doubting that. But tell me, Brauer, how long do you think such a fine soul can survive in this corrupt world, with all its temptations? How long, without the guidance of Christ?"

"Tapioca doesn't need any Christ. He knows what's bad and what's good. And he knows because I taught him, Reverend."

"You're a good man. You've done all you can for the boy. Now you have to let Jesus take over."

The Gringo leaned back in his chair and lit a cigarette.

"Jesus!" he said and laughed through clenched teeth. "When Tapioca was left here, he was like a baby animal abandoned by its mother. And I don't mean a pup. I raised all these dogs from pups: give them a bit of food and a pat and the next day they follow you around wagging their tails. No. Tapioca was like a little wild animal, a pampas cat: timid and wary. It took me months to get his trust and affection. I know him like the palm of my hand. And believe me, he doesn't need any Jesus Christ. And he doesn't need some John the Baptist like you to come along with your snake-oil spiel and tell him about the end of the world and all that crap."

The Reverend took another sip, playing for time. He knew about men like Brauer. Men who were basically good but hadn't let Christ into their lives. Men who lived from day to day, trusting their instincts, never realizing they were part of a bigger plan. If you didn't want to get them offside, you had to watch your step. Brauer had obviously graduated from the school of hard knocks. The Reverend himself might have lived like that if not for his collision with Christ on the riverbank that afternoon so many years before. Men like Brauer were a real challenge for him.

"I understand," he said.

The Gringo examined him, keeping his guard up.

"I understand completely. I apologize for interfering. Do you have a little more beer? It's been so long since I had a drink, I'd forgotten how delicious it is. After all, if God put it on earth, it has to be good, don't you think?"

The two men finished their beer in silence.

"The wind is changing," said Brauer, standing up and stepping out from under the awning.

The Reverend got up from his chair too and went to stand beside the mechanic. They looked at the sky.

"Do you think it might rain?" asked Pearson.

"No. They didn't say anything on the radio. Bit of blustery wind, that's all. I'm going to get back to it, Pearson."

"Sure, sure."

The Gringo walked away slowly, followed by one of the dogs. He took the rag that he always kept tucked into his belt to wipe his hands on and began to flick it in the air. On for a game, the dog stopped in his tracks and started jumping up to grab the piece of cloth. The Gringo waved it higher and higher, up to the level of his own head. The dog kept jumping and barking, baring his teeth, until he managed to snatch the rag and run away. The mechanic ran after him for a few yards but then had to stop, coughing his lungs out.

The Reverend had been watching the scene with a smile, but he was alarmed by the sight of Brauer bent double and coughing like that.

"Are you all right?" he called out.

Hands on his knees, hawking and spitting out threads of saliva, the Gringo lifted an arm to signal that he was all right, no need to worry. When the fit was over, he wiped his mouth on his arm.

"You watch out, you mongrel," he shouted at the animal, who had flopped down near the Reverend's car with the rag still in his mouth, wagging his tail.

Pearson decided to stretch his legs. The beer had made him feel woozy and he needed to clear his head. He climbed up onto the verge and began to walk along beside the empty road. The top buttons of his shirt were undone, and the hot wind blew in and filled it out, making him look like a hunchback. He walked slowly, with his hands in his pockets.

The scene of the baptism came back to him again.

When his mother had thrown him, the Preacher had caught him in his cold, wet arms and kissed his forehead. He was frightened and kept his eyes fixed on his mother, who was smiling at him from a few yards away. He was scared that she might vanish into the crowd and abandon him forever.

He had heard stories like that. His grandmother had told him that once, when she was waiting for the train, a woman had come up to her with a baby wrapped in a blanket. The woman asked her if she could hold the baby while she went to the bathroom. His grandmother said yes, take your time. When the train blew its whistle coming into the station, the woman still hadn't returned. So his grandmother left the baby with a policeman and boarded the train. She never found out what had happened: had the mother come back or had it all been a trick to get rid of the child? She kept looking out the window until the train pulled out and the platform shrank away, but there was no sign of the woman.

When the Preacher tried to give the boy back to his mother, she raised her arms and cried out:

"Praise be to Jesus! And praise to the Prophet who speaks in his name!"

The group of believers went crazy; all at once they raised their arms, forming a great human wave, begging the Prophet to speak to them in the tongue of Christ.

So he had no choice but to give his sermon with the child still in his arms. And the child being solidly built, the Preacher had to keep shifting the weight from side to side. With each shift, the boy had a different view of the group that had gathered on the beach to listen.

Gradually he got over his fear and began to enjoy the attention: so many pairs of eyes fixed on him (although, in fact, they were looking at the Prophet), so many faces, rapt or smiling or even crying, but all giving off so much love.

That afternoon, the Preacher spoke of choosing Christ over everything, and deciding to change the rest of one's life. A lot of it went over the boy's head: he was still little; there were words he didn't know. But it made a deep impression on him: the sermon, the way the words were arranged, and the different effects they had on the audience.

For example, a woman came running from the back and threw

herself face down in the mud of the riverbank, reaching out to the Preacher's feet and crawling up to kiss them.

A man cried out that Jesus was coming into his heart; he could feel a burning inside him, as if he were having a heart attack. He tore off his shirt and started spinning around with his arms outstretched, like a human windmill, striking whatever came into his range, whirling and shouting: "Jesus has taken me! Praise him!"

An old man who seemed to have seen it all before began to shout that the Preacher was a liar, a false prophet, and that he could prove it. But that was all he got to say, because he was attacked by a group of believers, including women, who beat him with their purses or whatever they happened to be holding.

After all those strange outbursts, the Preacher called the faithful to order and addressed himself to those who were not yet saved but ready to welcome Christ into their hearts. He asked them to form a line. A group, no doubt made up of his assistants, began to sing beautiful songs while marshaling the crowd.

He saw that his mother had joined the line.

When everything was ready, the Preacher retraced his steps, walking back into the river until it was up to his waist. Suddenly, the boy felt his feet go into the water and he was afraid. He looked for his mother again, but this time he couldn't see her in that mass of heads lined up one behind the other. He began to struggle and kick at the Preacher's bony hips. The man told him, softly, to keep still, then gripped him under the arms and held him aloft. Up in the air, he kept flailing his limbs and his eyes filled with tears. The next thing he knew, his whole body was plunged into the dense, black water. All he could do was shut his mouth and hold his breath. It could only have lasted a couple of seconds, but still, in that time, he thought he would die. And then, all at once, he was out again, coughing and spitting. Someone took him and carried him to the beach. He was left lying face up on the dirty sand that smelled of rotten fish, looking at the leaden sky, his clothes soaked and his body chilled, a stream of warm piss running over his legs.

Other bodies started dropping beside him, soaking wet, with their hair slicked down. Some just lay there; others sat up and wrapped their arms around their knees, shivering and singing.

He got up and started walking through the crowd. They all looked like the survivors of a shipwreck. Finally, he found his mother, coming out of the river with the help of two women, coughing and pale; she was scared of the water.

He ran to her and threw his arms around her waist.

14

Tapioca crawled into the shell of a car. He felt the springs stick-
ing into his back and shifted on the seat until he was comfortable. Whenever he wanted to be alone and think about things,
he got in among the wrecks. It was a habit that went back to his
first days there. When he was ashamed to let the Gringo see him
crying because he missed his mother, he would hide in one of
the old cars. Sometimes not even the dogs could find him.

Now he wanted to think about everything the Reverend had
said. Not all of it was new to him: when he was little, his mother
had told him about God and the angels; she had even taught him
some prayers, which he'd forgotten since. In the room where
they slept, they had a picture of La Difunta Correa, with a light
inside, and at night his mother would switch it on so he wouldn't
be afraid of the dark.

Over the years he had often thought of that picture. When he
first came to live with the Gringo, he would shut his eyes, alone
in his bed, and the memory of that little image would appear,
with its tiny light no brighter than a firefly. It was like having
his mother there, because La Difunta was a mother too; she had
a baby attached to her breast; she was already dead but the milk
kept coming to feed her little child. Years later, at the beginning

of his adolescence, the image came back to him again, but without the child: the woman stretched out on the ground with her breasts exposed. Afterward, he felt dirty and full of shame.

It might not have been as clear or precise in Tapioca's mind as what the Reverend had said, but for some time now he had been feeling something similar. He couldn't explain it and would never have dared to tell anyone, but he could often hear a voice. It wasn't coming from outside. And it wasn't just in his head. It was a voice that seemed to surge up from his whole body. He couldn't make out what it said, but every time it happened he felt comforted.

Thinking things over now, he realized that it was a voice like the Reverend's, filling him with confidence and something else he couldn't yet name. Was it possible that Pearson had been speaking to him from a distance, sending a message to say he was coming, on those nights when Tapioca couldn't sleep, and was overcome, as he lay there in the dark, by a feeling of peace and plenitude?

He didn't know. After hearing that nocturnal voice, he would wake up in the grip of an inexplicable happiness. He had never mentioned any of this to the Gringo. His boss might not have understood, but the real reason the boy kept quiet was that he felt he had something of his own for once. It frightened him sometimes, too. Something so big and powerful and impossible to explain: What was he meant do with it?

The Reverend had ended up there for a reason. He had come to help. Tapioca could tell him his secret.

He found himself wishing the Gringo would never fix the car, so that the man and his daughter would stay with them forever. What would become of him when they left? He wasn't a little kid anymore; he wasn't going to run after their car and howl, like he did when the truck took his mother away.

"Take me for a spin?"

Leni's voice startled him. He saw the girl's head appear on the passenger side of the car. He felt the blood rushing to his face, as if he had been caught with his hand in the cookie jar.

Without waiting for an invitation, she crouched down and eased herself onto the busted-up seat. Her knees were level with her chest.

Two dogs crawled in through the gap where the rear windshield had been and settled down on what was left of the back seat.

Soft yellow grass grew under the chassis. Leni took off her shoes and plunged her feet into that cool mat.

Around the frame of the front windshield, there were still some pieces of shattered glass. The wipers were suspended in midair. They looked like the antennae of a giant insect whose head was hidden under the hood.

There were other wrecked cars in front of them, some in worse shape than the one they were in. Leni felt like they were stuck in a traffic jam of phantom cars, on a highway leading straight to hell.

She told Tapioca, but he wasn't amused.

"I wouldn't like to go to hell," he said seriously.

"Where would you like to go then?" she asked.

"I don't know. Heaven, maybe. What you said at the table, about heaven, it sounds like a beautiful place, doesn't it?"

Leni stifled a giggle.

"But you have to be dead before you can go to heaven. Do you really want to die?"

"No. First I'd like to see my mother."

"Where is she?"

"In Rosario."

"Why don't you go and see her? Rosario's not that far from here."

"I don't know where she lives. Do you know Rosario?"

"Yes. My father and I go there sometimes."

"Is it big?"

"Sure is. A big city, with tall buildings and lots of people."

Tapioca rested his arms on the steering wheel. It seemed to Leni that he had grown sad; maybe he was thinking that he'd never be able to find his mother in such a big place. She thought about telling him that she too had lost her mother, to comfort him, but her father wouldn't have liked that, and it would have made her sad as well.

"Do you know what happened to this car?" she asked, to change the subject.

"Yes, a head-on smash on the highway, with another car. The other one crumpled up like an accordion, you should have seen it. It was brand-new. They make them out of plastic these days. This one wasn't so badly damaged because it's an old model; they're tougher."

"And did someone die?"

"I don't know. They might have been lucky." Tapioca paused. "If someone dies suddenly, in an accident, say, do they go straight to heaven?"

"I guess so, if they were good."

The two of them sat there in silence. Leni rested her arm on the window frame and leaned back in the seat. She could feel the springs pressing into the sweaty skin of her back. She closed her eyes.

One day she would get in a car and leave it all behind for good. Her father, the church, the hotels. She might not even look for her mother. She would just drive straight ahead, following the black ribbon of asphalt, putting it all behind her forever.

15

The Reverend stopped walking and wiped his neck and chest with his handkerchief. The wind, blowing hot as the Devil's breath, gave no relief at all. He sat down on the roadside embankment. Dry grass stems pushed through the fabric of his trousers and into his soft flesh. He stretched out his legs and rested his hands on the ground.

With Tapioca, everything would be different. The Reverend would not abandon the boy as the Preacher had abandoned him. He would be a true guide, forging the boy's character in accordance with the will of Christ, not the will of the church.

Over the years, he had sown the seed in the souls of many men. Good men like Pastor Zack, who did their best, which was often far more than he had imagined they could do. But they were all men with a past, and each one had his weaknesses. Day after day, the Reverend knew, they had to struggle against temptation. With Christ's help, they resisted, and carried on, but everything always seemed to be hanging by a thread.

He loved those men, God bless them; without their help, his work could not have prospered. He had gone behind the church's back and trained his own pastors. He had sought them out in places that were barely marked on the map, where nobody else dared to venture, in the small communities forgotten by the government and organized religion.

He had taken those men from their human misery and raised them up to Christ. He trusted them, but he remembered where they came from. They had all been stray sheep, in the grip of sin; each one of them had been through his own personal hell on earth. Jesus was running in their veins now. Their minds, their hearts, and their hands were clean. They were bearers of Christ's word and they knew their responsibilities. But whoever has been tempted once by the Devil can fall back into temptation. Sin is a tumor whose growth can be slowed; it can even be cut out. But once it has colonized a body, there is always a chance that it has left a little root somewhere, waiting to grow again when conditions are right.

Tapioca, on the other hand, was as clean as a newborn child; all his pores were open, ready to take Jesus in and breathe him out again.

Together they would turn the Reverend's work, which was still just the sketch of a long-cherished dream, into something concrete and monumental.

Tapioca, José, would not be his successor, but what the Reverend had failed to become. Because Reverend Pearson had a past too, as he knew better than anyone else, and in that past there were mistakes, and those mistakes came back now and then to haunt him like a vague but persistent cloud of buzzing flies. There had been no Reverend Pearson to guide him. He had fashioned himself as best he could. But the boy would have him. With Reverend Pearson on one side and Christ on the other, José would be invincible.

With difficulty, he got to his feet. He brushed the earth and dry grass stems from his trousers and his hands. He needed a bath and clean clothes and a soft bed. But there would be time

for that, later on. Now he had to convince Brauer to let him take
the boy with them to Castelli. Just a couple of days, he would say,
and then I'll bring him back. He would find some way to bring
the mechanic around.

A couple of days would be enough to show the boy the magnificent destiny that Christ had in store for him.

This is the moment to change your lives forever. Many of you, I'm sure, go to bed each night thinking: Tomorrow it will all be different; starting from tomorrow, I'm going to take the bull by the horns, I'm going to do all those things I've been putting off for years. Tomorrow, yes, tomorrow I'll change the course of my life. Tomorrow I'm going to fix the window that has been broken for years now, letting in the cold and rain in winter, and in summer the heat and the flies. Tomorrow I'm going to weed the yard and plant seeds so we'll have vegetables to eat this year. Tomorrow I'm going to leave this man I have for a husband, who does nothing but abuse me and my children. Tomorrow I'm going to make peace with my neighbor; we haven't spoken for decades, and I can't even remember why we fought. Tomorrow I'll look for a better job, and find one. Tomorrow I'm going to stop drinking. Tomorrow. In the evening, we are all optimists. We think that when the light of a new day fills the sky above us, we will be able to change everything and begin afresh. But the next morning we wake up exhausted, tired before we start the day, and we leave it all to tomorrow again. And tomorrow is no longer twenty-four hours long. Tomorrow ends up being years and years of the same misery.

I say to you: Tomorrow is now.

Why let time pass, winter with its frosts, summer with its storms? Why keep watching life go by from the edge of the road? We are not cattle watching it all from behind a fence, waiting for the truck to come and take us to the slaughterhouse.

We are people who can think, feel, and choose our own destiny. All of you can change the world.

You might be thinking: Reverend, my back is broken from working so hard to scrape a bit of money together and feed my family. Or: Reverend, I have grown old from bearing so many children, from so much sweat and strain. Or: Reverend, I am ill and I can't even look after myself. Reverend Pearson is a fool; what he's asking us to do is impossible, that's what you might be saying to yourselves. The Reverend comes here and talks to us and fills us with hope, and then he goes off and leaves us alone and we have to deal with our lives.

And that's where you're wrong. You're not alone. You will never be alone if you have Christ in your heart. You'll never be tired or ill again if you take Christ with you. Christ is the best vitamin you can give your body. Let Christ live in you and you'll have strength and energy and the power to change the direction of your life.

Together we are going to change the world. Together we are going to make the earth a fairer place where the last will be first. And we're not going to wait until tomorrow. Tomorrow is today. Today is the big day. Today is the day to make the big decision in your life.

Open your hearts and let Christ in!

Open your minds and let his word in!

Open your eyes and see the wonderful life that begins today, here, right now, for all of you, God bless you!

16

The reddish-yellow dog sat up suddenly on his hind legs. He had spent the whole day lying in a pit dug early that morning. Cool at first, the hole had gradually warmed up under his sprawling body.

Yellow was a greyhound cross, with the elegance, the height, the vigor, and the quick, slender legs of that breed. From his mother's or his father's side he had inherited a coat of coarse, longish yellow fur and a little beard that covered the end of his muzzle and gave him the air of a Russian general. And he was sometimes called Ruski, but only because of the color of his fur. Decades and decades of interbreeding had perfected his sensitivity. Or perhaps it was unique to him, an individual trait, why not? Why shouldn't animals have them too? He was, in any case, a particularly sensitive dog.

Although he had barely used his muscles, lying still all day, the blood that went on coursing through his body had made the pit so hot not even the fleas could stand it anymore: hopping like bears on a plate of hot iron, they had quit this dog for another, or the dirt, where they lay in wait for a more amenable host to come along.

But it wasn't the fleas deserting him that made Yellow sit up suddenly. Something else had roused him from his dry, hot drowsiness and brought him back into the world of the living.

Yellow's caramel-colored eyes were full of sleep, clouded still by a fine film that distorted his vision. But he didn't need his vision now.

Without shifting from the pit, he raised his head slightly. Two or three times, in rapid succession, the sensitive nostrils at the tip of his pointed snout sampled the air. He lowered his head, waited a moment, and then began sniffing again.

That smell was many smells together. Smells that came from far away, which had to be teased apart, identified, and recombined in order to reveal what it was, that smell made up of mixtures.

There was the smell of the depths of the forest. Not its heart but something much deeper, the bowels, you might say. The smell of the earth's dampness under the excrement of animals, the microcosm seething there beneath the dung: tiny seeds, minuscule insects, and blue scorpions, the lords and masters of that little dark plot.

The smell of feathers rotting in abandoned nests, along with sticks and leaves and animal fur.

The woody smell of a tree struck by lightning and burnt to the core, invaded by tunneling grubs and termites, and woodpeckers puncturing the dead bark to eat any living thing they could find.

The smell of big mammals: honey bears, foxes, pampas cats; in heat, or giving birth, or rotted down to skeletons.

From beyond the forest, out on the plain, the smell of the anthills.

The smell of musty shacks, full of *vinchuca* bugs. The smell of smoke from crackling fires under the eaves, and the smell of the food being cooked on them. The smell of the cakes of soap that women use for washing clothes. The smell of wet clothes drying on the line.

The smell of the day laborers bent double in the cotton fields. The smell of the plantations. The smell of fuel from the threshers.

And closer by, the smell of the nearest town, with its cemetery on the outskirts and the garbage dump half a mile out, and its unsewered neighborhoods with their cesspits and wastewater. And the smell of the passion fruit vine stubbornly climbing posts and wires, filling the air with the sweet scent of its sticky fruit, whose nectar brings the flies.

Yellow shook his head, overwhelmed by all those recognizable smells. He scratched his muzzle with a paw, as if to clear and cleanse his nose.

The smell that was all those smells was the smell of the coming storm. Even though the sky was still perfectly cloudless and clear, as blue as the sky in a postcard.

Yellow lifted his head again, half opened his jaws, and let out a very long howl.

The storm was on its way.

17

The Gringo turned the key in the ignition, and the car's motor purred like a snuggling cat. He gave a joyful yell and punched the inside of the roof with both fists. Then he got out and stood in front of the open hood with his hands on his hips, unable to wipe the smile off his face.

"Thought you were going to beat me, didn't you? Well, take that," he said to the motor, which was still humming softly, and flipped it the bird.

He lit a cigarette and looked around for someone to share his triumph with.

No one. Not even a dog. Where could they have gotten to? He went back to the car, reaching one arm under the steering wheel, and turned the motor off.

That was when he heard the sharp, plaintive howl, and a chilly tingle ran across his back.

Damn dog. Gave me a scare. What's that about, howling at this time of day? Looking for some action?

He headed for the house. Now he was going to sit himself down and drink all the beer in the fridge: he'd earned it. There was always plenty of beer. Since they lived a long way from town, the guy from the wholesaler came by once a week and dropped off three whole crates. With this heat, the Gringo needed a good supply. He drank it just like water. If he wanted to get hammered, there was whiskey, but for taking it nice and easy, beer was fine.

He hardly ever got really drunk. Over the years, alcohol had started to make him touchy and aggressive. Even when he'd been young, it had put him in a fighting mood, but then he could still look after himself, he was still quick with his fists. Now that he was getting on, he had to keep out of trouble. Bar fights weren't what they used to be. Before, when things got out of hand, it might have been settled at knifepoint. Now, any little shit could pull out a piece and blow you away just like that, for nothing.

If he wanted to tie one on, and he did sometimes, because it feels great, especially at first, when you're so happy you dance by yourself, he'd stay home and put away one of the bottles of JB the police gave him every now and then, as a bonus, for all his hard work. He'd pull the table out from under the awning, sit himself down, open the bottle, and stay there until it was finished. He'd put on a *chamamé* cassette and call Tapioca to come sit with him. He didn't let the kid have whiskey, but he'd offer him a glass of beer or two.

They would look up at the stars in silence, what silence the music left. And they would watch what traffic there was: cars full of kids on their way to the dance, if it was a weekend; or trucks setting off on their trips in the cool of the evening; or a bold hare crossing the road, stopping on the verge to stare at them for a moment with its shining eyes. Then Brauer would start talking to himself, though he could never remember what he said. Tapioca would stay there, like a soldier at his post, but maybe he wasn't even listening.

The Gringo was probably reminiscing. Talking about the old days when he was young and strong as an oak: drinking till the sun came up, getting himself into girl trouble. As a young man, he'd been something to look at: women would offer themselves to him, and he could service several in one night, so as not to give any cause for envy. He rarely felt like it anymore. Just as his muscles had gone soft, getting it up was an exercise he practiced less and less often.

It would take him several hours to empty the bottle, and in that time he would only leave the table to walk a few steps away and take a piss. Tapioca would fetch the ice, and when the cassette came to the end, he'd turn it over or change it.

After the last gulp of whiskey, Brauer would slam the horn cup down on the tabletop. He'd wake up the next day, well into the morning, on his bed, still dressed.

Now as he walked past the old gas pump, Yellow groaned, dropping from his upright howling position, stretching out his front paws and shaking his haunches.

"What's up, Ruski? Don't tell me you're in *love*," he said, ruffling the dog's head on his way to the open door.

18

When the Gringo came out again, wearing a clean shirt and holding a cold bottle of Quilmes, it was getting dark.

Only a few minutes had passed.

"What the fuck?" he said, stepping out from the porch.

Fat, gray, heavy clouds had filled the sky. They were full of wind and lightning and hopefully rain as well. The storm had gathered in the blink of an eye.

If they hadn't needed the rain so badly, the Gringo would have stopped it like his mother taught him, because it wasn't looking pretty. She had passed the *secret* on to him before she died. Out in the open, facing the storm front, you drive an ax into the ground six times, to make three crosses, and after the last blow you leave it stuck there. It's hard to believe if you've never seen it done, but the sky opens and the raging storm turns into a blustery passing wind. The storm slinks off, with its tail between its legs, to someplace where no one knows the *secret*. But those who know it must use it with care. Every crack in the earth was crying out for rain. This was no time to turn a storm away.

Nature's *secret*, thought the Gringo, kills any secrets man can know.

He opened the bottle with his lighter and took a gulp. The wind was swirling up dirt. Plastic bags, pieces of paper, and small branches began to blow past.

Through the dust, he saw the Reverend come trotting down from the edge of the road. One by one, the dogs appeared, ten or twelve of them—Brauer had lost count—and huddled all together under the table. All except for Yellow, or Ruski, who stayed by his side, with his mouth half-open, baring his teeth at the increasingly black and angry sky.

The Gringo felt like letting out a whoop. His lungs had been shot for years, but somehow he summoned the breath and the strength to make the darkening afternoon resound with his cry. Yellow joined in with a long howl.

The wind was blowing the Reverend's thin hair about. He approached with his shirt hanging out and flapping behind him; the force of the wind had unbuttoned it, revealing his white, hairy belly.

He was smiling. He had his secret reasons to thank God for the storm. Joyfully, the Gringo put his arm around the Reverend's shoulder and handed him the bottle. Pearson drank from it without turning up his nose; and the two stood there, facing the storm as it came panting like a huge, wet, terrifying animal.

That was when Tapioca and Leni appeared: two skinny figures battling through the wind, their eyes and mouths full of dust, but smiling. The girl's hair was a total mess and her skirt blew up, showing her pale, firm thighs.

They were received into the embrace of that human barrier against the coming storm. All four raised their faces to the sky. Right then, nothing could have been better.

How long did it last? Who can say? In that unique moment of plenitude, the four of them were one. The bottle went from hand to hand until it was empty. Even Leni gave it a kiss without her father objecting.

The first drops began to fall, hard and cold. Then came a barrage, and the infantry squad ran for cover, retreating to the porch.

19

The rain came pounding down. The porch awning, made of leaves and branches, leaked all over, and fierce gusts of wind blew the rain in from the sides. But the four of them stayed out there for a while, watching the downpour, seeing how the thirsty earth absorbed the drops as soon as they hit the ground. It would have to rain for a couple of hours before any mud began to form.

Leni hugged herself. The temperature had barely fallen, but her clothes were wet, and the water dripping from her hair was running down her back. She couldn't remember a storm like this. Blue cracks flashed in the sky, giving the landscape a ghostly look.

Five hundred yards away, in a field, lightning struck a tree, and the orange flames held out against the rain for a good long while.

It was a beautiful spectacle. Sometimes the curtain of water was so dense they couldn't see the old gas pump, although it was just a few yards away.

The four of them were quiet, absorbed in their own private thoughts, until the Gringo said hoarsely:

"Let's go in."

The storm had cut off the electricity, so he used the little quivering flame of his lighter to guide him as he went looking for the packets of candles. He lit several and placed them around the room. Tapioca brought in some plastic chairs, which he dried, and they sat down around the kitchen table.

The roof began to leak in the middle of the room, and they put a pan there to catch the drip. Despite the racket of the rain on the tin, that regular, metallic sound was clearly audible.

The dogs had made themselves comfortable under one of the beds, except for Yellow, who was lying near the door.

"It's going to be a long night," said the Gringo.

He went to the fridge and took out some cold meat, a piece of cheese, and bread. Tapioca brought glasses and Cokes for himself and Leni. The men drank beer. They ate in silence. The excitement of the storm had made them hungry. The moment of communion outside, facing the elements, was followed, in the shelter of the house, by introspection.

The Reverend made no attempt to say grace. They ate as if they had returned from a hard day's work. Leni rarely had much of an appetite (it had been quite a struggle for Pearson to get her to touch her food after they left her mother), but now, inspired by the storm's voracity, she ate as much as the men.

When they finished all the food, and were full, Leni cleared the table, collecting the boards and knives and wiping away the crumbs with a rag. Assuming her role as the woman of the house, when the Gringo lit a cigarette, she duly brought him a clean ashtray.

She suggested they play cards, although she didn't know any games. Tapioca got a shoebox down from the top of a wardrobe. There was a pack of cards in it, along with dice, a cup, and a pile of photos. Brauer and the Reverend told the young ones to go ahead and play. Pearson, of course, frowned on games of chance, but he decided to let it pass, this once. The Gringo was right: the night would be long, and they might as well amuse themselves somehow until they were ready to sleep.

So Leni and Tapioca settled down at opposite ends of one of the beds, with the shoebox between them.

The Reverend and the Gringo remained seated at the little table, face-to-face, their knees almost touching underneath.

Nothing could be seen through the slightly open window. It was all completely black, except for when the lightning flashed. But nothing was visible then either: it all went completely white. The thunderstorm was blowing over: the lightning bolts were followed now by a muffled rumbling. The wind had dropped as well, but the rain continued, heavy and dense. After the long summer of drought, the earth was beginning to slake its thirst and regurgitate water, burping up bubbles, as if to say that's enough for a while.

The Gringo, who had seemed to be on another planet since the beginning of the meal, shook his head and said: "Did I say I got your car going?"

"No. That's great news."

"Yeah. Pity I didn't finish before the weather turned bad."

The Reverend smiled.

"Well, let's just be grateful we weren't on the road when the storm hit."

"True. That would have been tricky."

"You see what I mean: the Lord always has a reason for doing things the way he does."

"We're not going to start talking about God, Pearson," said the Gringo, gently shaking his head. "There's plenty of things you couldn't explain the reason why he does them like that. I'd run out of fingers pretty quick if I started counting them up."

"All right. You have your ideas."

"Yep. I have mine and you have yours."

The Reverend took a sip from his glass. Now that Brauer had started talking, he didn't want to break off the dialogue.

"What was wrong with the car in the end?"

"Damned if I know. I fixed up so much stuff it's like I built you a new motor from scratch. Mechanics, it's a mystery sometimes, like that Christ of yours and his ways," he said slyly.

The Reverend smiled again.

"Tell me, Brauer, what did you do before you became a mechanic?"

The Gringo lit a cigarette and leaned back on his chair. He blew the smoke straight up. He wasn't used to talking about himself. When he talked with other men it was about things that were happening there and then, in the present, and memories came up only because they were shared: Remember when? Opening up is something men like Brauer just don't do. Not even in unguarded moments, when they're in bed with a woman. Brauer never opened up. Or maybe when he was drunk, but the only person there to hear was Tapioca, and with the years of living together, Tapioca had become a part of him. Talking to the kid was like talking to himself.

That night, though, was different. There they were, trapped by the rain. And Pearson wanted to talk. Fair enough. Why sit there drinking and watching each other like a pair of wary dogs? The man was trying to start a conversation. He didn't seem like a bad sort. Although they lived in different worlds.

"Before I did my military service—that was in Bahía Blanca; I'd never been so cold in my life; from one kind of hell to the other, imagine it—before that, I worked with my father. We had a bar, in Villa Ángela, opposite the train station. It was open twenty-four hours a day. And during harvest, we were flat out. We didn't stop. We took turns sleeping. My father, my mother, and me—I don't have any brothers or sisters—and a waiter, who was always changing; we never had any luck there: some of the guys were good for a start, but soon enough they all got a taste for the drink. And there was so much in easy reach. My father worked the till, my mother cooked, and the waiter and me took orders from the tables and served drinks. I started working as soon as I could lift a bottle. My mother always wished she had a girl to help in the kitchen, but she was unlucky there too. After I was born, she couldn't have any more kids. She always wanted to take in a girl and bring her up as her own. Back then, the day laborers used to come with their families; they all worked in the cotton fields, and plenty would have been happy to let someone else raise one of their daughters. Lots of rich women who couldn't have children did a deal like that. But my father was always against it. He said blood was thicker than water, and one day out of the blue the kid would up and go back to her family, however good it was with us."

"Is that what you believe too?" said the Reverend, cutting in, thinking perhaps of his ex-wife and Leni.

"What?"

"That blood is thicker than water."

The Gringo thought of Tapioca, and what his mother had said when she left him.

"I don't know. We make our own destinies, that's what I believe. We know why we do what we do."

The Reverend shook his head and looked at the Gringo.

"So they had a bar and you worked with them," he said, picking up the thread.

Brauer got up and replaced the empty bottle with a full one.

"Uh-huh. Until I was drafted at eighteen. And then my life changed. I'd never left the town. We didn't even have time to go fishing. Mind you, I saw all sorts of things when I was working in the bar. It wasn't just workers who came in. My mother was a good cook and the place was open all day. So as well as the day laborers, there were the engineers from the railways and the cotton gins, the landowners, Indians blowing the bit of cash they had. Alcohol is a great leveler, you know. One time a couple of engineers who worked at La Chaco got into a fight. They sucked the whiskey up like sponges, the gringos. And that stuff was pure kerosene, believe me. We got it smuggled in from Paraguay, you can imagine what it was like. These two came in like friends and started putting it away. They were talking their language, so we didn't understand a thing. All of a sudden, for some reason, they started arguing. My old man never got involved unless it was turning really ugly. But the gringos left him no time to react. One of them suddenly pulled out a revolver and blew the other's brains out. All the customers were drunk that night, as usual, but they sobered up fast, I'm telling you. They sat there, white in the face, like ghosts. Even the cigarette smoke froze. The gringo who had fired the shot started trembling like a leaf; he wanted to put the barrel in his mouth, but he couldn't, he was shaking too much. My father took the gun off him, led him to the door, and gave him a little push. Off you go, mister, back to the residence and watch yourself, he said. Then he came back in and sent me to the police station. I went on my bike, and you might find this shocking, but I was excited; the mission made me feel important. The police came and took the body away. No one asked any questions. My mother wiped the gringos' table and cleaned up the brains spattered on the floor. My father said: 'A drink on the house for everyone, doctor's orders.' In five minutes, it was all in the past, and we were back to business. The customers drank even more than usual; I think they were celebrating their luck: they were just glad it hadn't been them."

The Gringo laughed. The Reverend drained his glass and pushed it forward to be refilled.

"Okay, now it's your turn," said the Gringo eagerly. It wasn't so bad after all, sharing memories. "How many men have you seen die?"

The Reverend put his lips to the edge of the glass and sipped at the froth, making a little noise that was drowned out by the din of rain on the tin roof. Then he wiped his face with his hand; his cheeks were rough with the day's stubble.

"Plenty. But all in their beds," he said, and they both smiled.

Pearson drank again; this time he broke through the barrier of foam and took a gulp of liquid.

"Although, when I was a kid, I saw a hanged man."

The Gringo leaned forward, intrigued.

"As a boy, I lived with my mother and my grandparents in their house. My father left us before I was born. Behind the house, at the back of the yard, there was a little room with a bathroom, which my grandfather let to an acquaintance. An old man, on his own, without any family. A bachelor. He'd been in the merchant navy and had a good pension, but he'd never started a family because he'd always been at sea. That was where he lived. We didn't have much to do with him. He came and went. He had his life outside. He went out a lot at night and slept during the day. I suspect he was a gambler. I was fascinated by him; he was quite a bit younger than my grandfather, more like my father, in age, at least. But he wasn't interested in children, so he paid no attention to me. Years later I learned that my father had been in the navy too, so I guess that was a sort of connection. Anyway, I was always looking for excuses to go to his room. Even if it meant annoying him. I'd kick a ball against the wall in the middle of the afternoon until he came out in his pajamas, with his hair all a mess, and gave me an earful. And I was satisfied with that. But sometimes my grandmother sent me to see him. If she was cooking something special, she'd always make an extra helping and ask me to take it out to him. One day, at lunchtime, she had made one of his favorite dishes, and she was about to send me out with the plate. Then we realized we hadn't seen him for a couple of days or noticed the scent of English aftershave that he left in the corridor when he went out. With the warm plate in my hands, I went to his door and knocked several times. Since there was no answer, I tried the handle. It wasn't locked, so I pushed the door open with my shoulder. The room was dark; the shutters were closed. As soon as I stepped in I smelled something sweet, disgusting, and unrecognizable. I put the plate down on the first surface I could find by feeling around. Then I felt for the light switch. The first thing I saw, at eye level, level with the eyes of a seven-year-old, were the shoes, handmade and shiny; then I looked up at the trousers, the tucked-in silk shirt, the jacket, the handkerchief in the breast pocket, the rope around his neck. For some reason my gaze went no higher than the knot but came down again to the slumped shoulders, the arms hanging limp, the shirt cuffs with their gem-studded cufflinks, partly covering the veined hands. I took two or three steps back and went out into the yard for some air. I knew and didn't know what was happening. I knew, but I didn't know how I would say it. The strangest thing is that I went back to the house and sat down at the table and ate up all the food on my plate. When I had swallowed the last mouthful, I threw it all up on the floor. And when I'd finished vomiting, I said to my grandfather: 'Go and see him; he's dead.'"

Pearson finished his story and took several gulps in a row. His mouth felt dry and his cheeks were burning. God knew how long it had been since he had thought about that incident. He might have told the story only once before, to Leni's mother, when they were courting, to impress her.

The Gringo was impressed too. As if seeing a man die right in front of you was less dramatic than finding one who has already taken his own life. Different kinds of shock, for sure, but the underlying question was the same: Why did the bachelor hang himself? Why did the engineer kill his colleague? What is death but the same dark, empty nothing, regardless of the hand that deals it?

20

Tapioca tried to show Leni a simple game to play with the Spanish cards. But she went straight for the photos in the shoebox. Where's the pleasure in looking at a bunch of pictures of people you don't even know? Tapioca, it seemed, had no idea what a girl's idea of fun might be.

He couldn't tell her about the photos, except for the four or five that showed him and the Gringo at the Bermejito river. There were brown pictures of Brauer's dead relatives. And one of a little kid who might have been his boss, maybe.

Leni grabbed the photo and examined it, then looked at Tapioca. It wasn't him, obviously—the image was more than forty years old—but there was a certain resemblance.

The Gringo and Leni's father were chatting away. She tried to listen, but because of the racket the rain was making and the softness of their voices, she couldn't catch more than the odd word. Something about drunks and a guy who hanged himself. They seemed to be getting on fine, in the end.

She had never seen her father like this. Just drinking and talking, taking it easy, not mentioning Jesus all the time. She liked the idea of her father just talking with an ordinary, rough sort of guy. But what would Reverend Pearson have thought?

It was her father she had to live with, most of the time anyway, but Reverend Pearson would not have approved of this fraternizing, not at all. He would have converted Brauer already. Her father couldn't do that on his own.

"Mr. Brauer," she said, and she had to call his name again to make him turn around. "Is this you?" she asked, holding up the little photograph.

In the dimness, at a distance, he couldn't see a thing, of course.

"Give me a look," he said, beckoning her.

She put the rest of the photos back in the box and came over to the table. The Gringo took the cardboard rectangle and raised it to his eyes.

"Yes. I must have been four," he said and passed the photo to Pearson, who looked at it and smiled affectionately.

"It's funny to think of being a kid," said the Gringo, lighting a cigarette.

"Recently I've been thinking a lot about when I was a boy," said Pearson.

"I've never seen a photo of you when you were little, Father."

"Really? There must be one around somewhere."

"Or one of me as a little girl either, now that I come to think of it."

"I've never been that keen on photos."

"Don't tell me you think they steal your soul," said the Gringo sarcastically.

The Reverend smiled and shrugged his shoulders.

"Aren't there any photos of me, Father?"

"There must be, Leni. We'll have a look tomorrow."

Leni went back and sat down on the bed. If there were photos of her, if she could find them, maybe her mother would be in one. Then she wouldn't have to worry about losing the memory of her face; whenever it began to fade, she'd have the image there to remind her.

"Almost all those photos belonged to my mother. When she died, I brought them here; I think that's the box she kept them in. I don't even know who most of the people are. Why do we keep photos, anyway? What really matters, after all, is what's in here," said the Gringo, tapping his forehead with a finger.

They were quiet for a while. The sound of the rain was so persistent that it had become a part of the silence.

Pearson felt that the moment had come to say what he wanted to say. And he spoke loud and clear to make sure that the Gringo would not be the only one to hear it.

"Listen, Brauer, I'd like Tapioca to come with us to Castelli."

Tapioca, who was playing solitaire, lifted his head when he heard his name.

"To Castelli? And what's Tapioca going to do in Castelli?"

"It'll just be for a couple of days. To see the place."

"He's seen it already. We've been there plenty of times, haven't we, kid?"

"What?" asked Tapioca, pretending not to have heard.

"We've been to Castelli quite a few times."

"Yes."

"All the better. He can show Leni around."

"Come on, Pearson, what's this about?"

The Gringo lit another cigarette and emptied his glass.

Now Pearson adopted a confidential tone and lowered his voice so that only Brauer could hear him.

"Look, my daughter's a difficult girl. We're not getting on too well. For some reason—I guess it's her age—she's become rebellious. She's always angry, always finding fault with me. But she's hit it off with Tapioca. She doesn't get on like that with anyone,

I mean it. I think he could be a good influence on her. Like I said, I've never known a heart as pure as his."

The Gringo laughed softly, shaking his head. He tilted his face back and blew a jet of smoke up into the air. Then he pushed his chair away from the table; the plastic legs scraped on the cement. He got up and fetched another beer from the fridge. He felt around under the counter and put some more bottles into the freezer. There wasn't much point because the power was still out. But there was still some ice on the walls, so the bottles would cool down a bit.

Some of the candles had already gone out; the others were guttering. He opened a new packet; he always had a good supply for situations like this. Blackouts were common in the area. He lit several candles and stuck them in the wax where the others had been. The yellowish light intensified suddenly.

He peered out through the window. Although it was still raining, the storm had continued on its way. He slid one pane open. The wind had dropped; there was just a cool breeze now. The candle flames fluttered but held out against the draft.

Fresh air began to circulate. Only then did they realize how hot it had become inside. Although their clothes had dried a little, they were still damp and sticky from the stuffiness.

Brauer filled the glasses again. As far as he was concerned, the conversation was over.

But Pearson wasn't prepared to leave it there.

"Tapioca's company will do Leni a world of good."

"We have a lot of work to do here, Pearson."

"Just for two days. I promise you. I'll bring him back Tuesday morning."

"No. It's not going to be possible."

Tapioca had been waiting for an invitation to join in the conversation again. Leni kept looking through the photos, but she too was following closely what was happening at the table.

"It will be good for him too, Brauer. He'll get to meet other kids his age, and talk with them. It's a very healthy environment. It'll be like a little vacation."

"Some place full of evangelical kids, going on about Jesus all day long. Give me a fucking break, Pearson."

"I could go. If you let me, Gringo," Tapioca stuttered from the bed.

Brauer paid no attention. He didn't even turn to look at him.

"See?" said the Reverend with a slight smile.

The Gringo picked up the bottle and went out onto the porch.

21

Yellow went out after him. He stretched out his front paws, shook his back, and let out a little yawn that sounded like a whimper. Then he sat down on the wet ground.

The Gringo set the bottle on the table awash with water and craned his head out from under the awning. It was still raining, but not with the force of the first hours. The rain was falling monotonously, as if discharging a duty, without enthusiasm. Every now and then there was a weak and noiseless flash of lightning.

The storm must have been over Tostado, or even farther south by now, moving faster than any new car. And it probably wasn't so wild anymore. As if tired out by the traveling.

The next day, on the radio, it would be all about the storm. Sheds blown down, crops destroyed, dead animals, and human victims too, for sure. Someone always got killed: a power pole came down, cables broke, and there was some poor soul who happened to be in the wrong place at just the wrong time. Farther north, one of the rivers would have flooded. That was how it always went. Punished by drought, and then by rain. As if the land couldn't stop acting up and had to be punished all the time. It never got any slack.

The Gringo swigged from the bottle and took a deep breath. Clean air at last, without the dirt that was always floating in it, getting into your nose and your lungs. That's why his lungs were ruined: breathing in all that lethal dust.

In a soft flash of lightning, he saw the shiny asphalt and the treetops washed clean, as if newborn; even the car bodies looked like new, ready to hit the road again.

But there was no point fooling himself. In the morning it would all be the same as before. The burning sun would soon obliterate any memory of the rain.

Nostalgia overtook him. In the damp and dark, he saw himself as a young man, using his sheer brawn to lift the front end of a tractor or haul it several yards with a chain as thick as his leg. It was almost like dragging a child's toy—everything was so easy then. He remembered his military service: fifty of them sleeping in a shed full of that young-male stink. In a few years he would be an old man. Nothing he could do about that, although he didn't like the thought.

"Brauer."

Pearson's voice startled him.

"Listen to me, please. I need you to understand."

"To understand what? Why don't you leave us alone?"

"You don't realize how special that boy is; there's a treasure in him."

"A treasure! What are you talking about, Pearson? Tapioca's a good kid. We agree about that. He's a good kid and soon he'll be a good man. No mystery there. Or maybe there is, for you. Maybe you're not so good yourself, if it seems unusual to you. Maybe you're not the sort of man you want us to think you are, Pearson."

"Tapioca is much more than a good person. He's a pure soul. Christ has marked him out."

"Cut the crap, will you?"

"It's the truth. Please believe me. The boy is destined for great things."

"Great things! And what do you mean by great things, Reverend? You wouldn't be talking about yourself there, would you? You might think you're some great thing, Pearson, but let me tell you: you're greatly fucking mistaken."

"There are destinies greater than ours, Brauer."

"Your car's ready. As soon as it's light, and it won't be long now, I want you to go. If it wasn't for your daughter, I'd have kicked you out a while back."

"Listen to me. I was like Tapioca when I was a boy. I was good, Brauer, but I didn't grow up right because I didn't have a guide. Christ is my guide, but there were times when I couldn't understand what he was telling me, because I was slow, and young, and all on my own. All the people I put my trust in, they left me on my own. They wanted something else from me. When I saw Tapioca, I saw myself forty years ago. Suddenly I understood what Christ had really destined me for: I was meant to find that boy and save him."

"Save him? Stop this bullshit. You're drunk, Reverend."

"No. You don't understand. Joseph raised Jesus, but he knew to let go of him when the time came. I'm asking you to have the same generosity. You have no idea of the destiny awaiting that boy. You're going to ruin it all."

"Fuck you," said the Gringo and raised the bottle to take another gulp.

Pearson gripped him by the shoulder. The Gringo reacted instinctively: his free hand flew out, and he shoved at the Reverend's chest with an open palm. Pearson stumbled and fell on his butt. The Gringo let go of the bottle, bent over, and picked him up by the collar of his shirt. At first he meant to help him up, but once Pearson was on his feet, he gave him another shove, out into the rain.

It looked as if the Reverend would fall again, but he managed to keep his balance. And then, without thinking, he clenched his fists and threw himself at Brauer. The Gringo was unprepared for this reaction; he slipped in the mud and tumbled over with Pearson on top of him. He tried to prize himself free, pushing up on his opponent's chest, but the Reverend had him by the hair. Pearson's twisted features crowded into his field of vision, and he could smell his hot, alcoholic breath.

"You fight like a woman," Brauer scoffed, although his head was still half-buried in the mud, and he couldn't get free.

Ashamed, the Reverend let go of Brauer's hair and drew back, straddling his hips, preparing to land a fresh blow. That momentary relaxation allowed Brauer to shove him off easily, like a piece of fluff.

Now the Gringo was angry for real. He let his feet sink into the mud of the yard until they were planted firmly. He got into position.

Two yards away, the Reverend did the same.

"Come on," said the Gringo, beckoning scornfully with the fingers of one hand, stirring him up. "I'm waiting."

Pearson saw red. He ran at the Gringo. Never having fought before, he didn't have a plan. Brauer received him with a cross to the jaw. Pearson felt as if his brain had jumped inside his skull. He saw white. Then he took a punch to the stomach, and everything went black.

When he opened his eyes, he didn't know how much time had passed: Brauer was leaning over him, with his hands resting on his knees and water dripping from his hair. He looked worried. Pearson smiled as he lifted his arms and gripped Brauer's neck with the force of a crane. The Gringo leaped back, trying to get free, and this lifted the Reverend to his feet. Brauer landed a punch in the region of the kidneys, where the Reverend was particularly sensitive. The wave of pain loosened Pearson's grip and released the Gringo, who took a few steps back, massaging his neck with one hand.

Brauer licked the water dripping from his mustache. He laughed.

"Where's Christ now?" he shouted. "Why hasn't he come to help you?"

"Don't be a fool," gasped the Reverend. "This is pointless. Tapioca will come with me whether you like it or not."

Hearing the other man say his boy's name kindled the Gringo's rage. He charged at Pearson with his head down and knocked him over. But the exertion set off a coughing fit. He began hacking convulsively, phlegm and spittle dripping from his open mouth as he struggled to get some air back into his lungs. Bent double, gripping his stomach with one hand, he used what strength he had left to kick the Reverend in the ribs. Then he fell down, on his side, still coughing. He propped himself up on one arm to keep his head out of the mud and coughed awhile longer until the fit subsided. Then he flopped on his back beside the Reverend, who was lying still, with his arms at his sides.

22

Alarmed by the barking, Tapioca and Leni had come out almost as soon as the fight had begun. Yellow was standing on the porch. Although the fur on his back was bristling slightly, he hadn't gone to his master's defense. He had stayed in his place, like a nervous spectator who knows that, much as he would like to, he can't climb through the ropes and change the course of the fight. All he could do was heckle one of the contestants with his growling, and run back and forth across the porch, under the little awning of leaves, not stepping out into the mud.

Leni and Tapioca stayed on the sidelines too.

Leni crossed her arms, said nothing, and watched the fight unfold. She was like a bored onlooker at a boxing trial, wasting no energy on the undercard, saving her passion for the moment when the real champions would step into the ring. And yet, at some point, she began to cry. Just tears, without any sound. Water falling from her eyes as it was falling from the sky. Rain disappearing into rain.

Tapioca put his hands in his pockets. He had gone pale and kept shifting his weight from one foot to the other. He was scared that the Gringo and the Reverend would get injured. But he knew he couldn't step in. It was out of his hands, although he'd been the pretext for the fight. It was between the two of them, and really had nothing to do with him. In the end, they didn't care what he wanted.

And whether the Gringo liked it or not, what he wanted had something to do with what the Reverend was promising him. Not because of the Reverend and his promise, but because there was something inside him that was crying out for it. It was the voice calling him to Christ's side. The same voice he had heard in the bowels of the forest, and at night, in his bed, when the Gringo was sleeping, and he lay there with his eyes open. The voice that he had just discovered how to understand.

The boy, the girl, and the dog watched the trading of blows, the rolling in the mud, and the flailing about, due to drink-dulled reflexes and inexperience. They saw the men fall to the ground and lie there looking up at the sky, which was gradually brightening as day began to show through the veils of rain.

Now the rain was coming down lazily; it had thinned to a persistent drizzle.

Leni wiped her cheeks with her hands and went out into the yard. Yellow followed her gingerly, muscles tensed. He wagged his tail a little and licked his master's face. Brauer lifted his muddy hand and ran it over the dog's clean fur. Tapioca came out too, and between them they helped the men to their feet.

Back inside, Leni put the kettle on. Fuming, she stood there, arms crossed, with her back to the others, staring at the gas ring's blue flame. She was biting her lips, and her nostrils were trembling. When the water boiled, the whistle brought her back. She wiped her brow and started opening containers, looking for the coffee.

"Here," said Tapioca, handing her a jar. She put some in a pan and poured the water over it. A smell of fresh coffee filled the kitchen immediately.

The rain was falling softly; it had almost faded away.

Brauer and the Reverend were slumped on their chairs, in their wet, mud-covered clothes. The bruises hadn't yet appeared, but how their bodies ached. They were too old for that sort of thing.

Pearson touched his ribs, where the Gringo had landed his last kick. Nothing was broken, but he felt a sharp pain when he breathed deeply. His lip was swollen and he had no idea where his glasses had ended up. Slowly, he unbuttoned his shirt.

Tapioca handed them each a towel. The Reverend covered himself; he thought it improper to remain half-naked in the presence of his daughter. And he wasn't proud of the spectacle he had made of himself outside. God would be able to forgive him. But not Leni; she wasn't even looking at him. Just as well. He could imagine the scorn in her eyes, but he didn't think he could bear it, not yet.

The click of the lighter was clearly audible, it was now so quiet inside and out. The smell of tobacco smoke mingled with the scent of the coffee that Leni was pouring into mugs on the table.

Tapioca took a corner of the towel that the Gringo had slung over his shoulder and began to dry his boss's hair, rubbing quickly and firmly. Brauer felt like an old man, or a child again, which is not so different, except that in old age all the hopes and possibilities are gone. He had never given much thought to tomorrow or wondered how his days would end; he had always been a man of action, living in the here and now. Maybe Tapioca turning up had kept him from worrying. He didn't know. But now, as the kid rubbed his head with the towel, he felt diminished by this attention and understood that the kid was a man and had the right to choose for himself, just like he had done at that age. It was the way of things; no point resisting, he knew that.

"I'm going to Castelli," said Tapioca firmly.

The Gringo nodded.

Pearson smiled inwardly and took a sip of the hot, bitter coffee. Careful, he thought, pride is a beguiling sin.

"And I'm staying here," said Leni, in a loud, trembling voice. All three of them looked at her; she blushed. She didn't know why she had said such a thing. She was furious and wanted to punish her father and had said the first thing that came into her head. Now there was no way back, so she drew herself up and repeated:

"I'm staying here . . . for a while."

Suddenly she remembered her mother running after the car like an abandoned puppy. Her father, Reverend Pearson, had stepped on the accelerator and not even looked in the rearview mirror for a last glimpse of the woman who had been his wife and the mother of his child. She knew he could do it again, with her, and she was afraid.

"Don't talk nonsense," he said, cutting her off sharply.

"He's right, kid, you can't stay here. I never had . . ." the Gringo began, and then fell silent. I never had children so I wouldn't have problems, he had been about to say. But he didn't know what Tapioca's mother had told the boy; maybe he knew and was just playing dumb, being tactful. Better shut it, Gringo; the waters are muddy enough as it is. "There's only room here for me and the dogs," he said loud and clear, and looked at Tapioca apologetically.

The boy lowered his eyes and felt a lump swelling in his throat. He went to the wardrobe and started putting clothes in a bag. The same little bag with which he had arrived.

23

Soon the car shrank down to a metallic glint on the still-wet asphalt.

The Reverend didn't see it: he was driving, hunched over the steering wheel, peering shortsightedly without his glasses, his body aching from the blows. Moist air blew in through the open windows; the sounds of wind and speed filled the silence. He was happy, although his smile was hidden by the fold of his swollen lip. Blessed Jesus, his heart was almost jumping out of his chest. He took his eyes off the road only to steal a few glances at the boy beside him, all keyed up like a dog in a dinghy.

Tapioca didn't see it. He put his head out of the window and watched the house and the old gas pump getting smaller until they disappeared completely. He waited for the Gringo to appear in the picture, surrounded by the dogs, and raise his arm and wave his hand from side to side to say good-bye. But there was no sign of his boss or the dogs, as if the house where he had finished growing up was already a ruin.

Leni didn't see it. As soon as she got into the car, she stretched out to her full length on the back seat and covered her eyes with her arm. She wasn't going to look through the rear windshield like that time when they left her mother behind; she wasn't going to watch it all shrinking in the distance. She closed her eyes and begged Jesus, if he existed, to strike her dead with a lightning bolt. While she was waiting, she fell asleep.

Yellow didn't see it. He jumped straight up onto Tapioca's bed and turned around as many times as a dog needs to turn before lying down, and slept with his muzzle between his paws, making a regular sucking noise with his tongue, as if he were drinking his mother's milk.

And the Gringo didn't see it either. After letting his boy give him a hug, he slapped him twice on the back, firmly broke the embrace, and sent him on his way with a little push. And he didn't come out to watch them go. He was left on his own to work and get drunk and feed the dogs and die. Enough to keep him busy for a while. So he needed a bit of sleep before he set to it again.

SELVA ALMADA was born in Entre Ríos, Argentina, in 1973. She has been a finalist for the Rodolfo Walsh and Tigre Juan prizes, and is considered one of the most potent and promising literary voices in Argentina and Latin America.

CHRIS ANDREWS was born in Newcastle, Australia, in 1962. He has translated books by Roberto Bolaño and César Aira, among others. He teaches at the University of Western Sydney, where he is a member of the Writing and Society Research Center.

The text of *The Wind That Lays Waste* is set in Adobe Caslon Pro. Book design by Rachel Holscher. Composition by Bookmobile Design and Digital Publisher Services, Minneapolis, Minnesota. Manufactured by Versa Press on acid-free, 30 percent postconsumer wastepaper.